Advance praise for

Y

"A first-rate, literary novel, brilliantly written by a poet who knows how to make her heroine tangible, memorable, on fire. This is the kind of grown-up lesbian novel we've been waiting for. A shrewd, intimate, affirming look at lesbian life as it is really lived these days. I expect to see it on staff-pick tables in Borders and Barnes & Noble as well as on the bedside tables of young lesbians who need to revel in a sophisticated story about a real woman."

–Anne Kaier, PhD, Harvard University
Writer

"*Yin Fire* chronicles one intense woman's desire to be taken care of, to be visible to others and herself, laying bare the feelings and questions we've all puzzled over. . . . Driving towards the reunion of self and center."

–Nancy Welsh, President 2000/2001
Bay Area Career Women (BACW), San Francisco, California

"Powerful and poetic . . . takes the reader into the mind of a creative woman on a quest for wholeness. In the tradition of Faulkner and Morrison, Grilikhes lets us experience her lead character's intensity–the fear, anger, longing, and determination of one cast on the margin of society not only because of her status as woman, Jew, and lesbian, but by virtue of her reflexive refusal, despite repeated batterings, to efface her individuality."

–Charlotte Haines, PhD, Assistant Professor
Delaware County Community College, Pennsylvania

"In this intense novel of self-definition, we enter the world of Greek myth and Chinese medicine guided by the main character looking for the powerful, mist-surrounded goddess, the Mistress of the Animals. In this search . . . the beautiful acupuncturist and herbal specialist, Hongwei, is compelling."

–Elizabeth Floyd-Cameron, MA, MFA, Professor of Humanities
Moore College of Art & Design, Philadelphia

"A thrilling novel of a woman's love for women in all its exquisite and explicit detail. . . . A rhapsody in exoticism. . . . The narrative swirls and rivets the reader into the depths of relation-ships and in particular the life journey of the protagonist. It is exquisite. It is a learning experience. It is poetic joy."

–Georgiana Peacher, PhD, Professor Emerita
John Jay College, New York City

Yin Fire

Alice Street Editions
Judith P. Stelboum
Editor-in-Chief

Yin Fire, by Alexandra Grilikhes

His Hands, His Tools, His Sex, His Dress: Lesbian Writers on Their Fathers, edited by Catherine Reid and Holly K. Iglesias

Weeding at Dawn: A Lesbian Country Life, by Hawk Madrone

Façades, by Alex Marcoux

Inside Out, by Juliet Carrera

Past Perfect, by Judith P. Stelboum

Forthcoming

Treat, by Angie Vicars

From Flitch to Ash: A Musing on Trees and Carving, by Diane Derrick

To the Edge, by Cameron Abbott

Egret, by Helen Collins

Back to Salem, by Alex Marcoux

Extraordinary Couples, Ordinary Lives, by Lynn Haley-Banez and Joanne Garrett

Foreword

Alice Street Editions provides a voice for established as well as up-and-coming lesbian writers, reflecting the diversity of lesbian interests, ethnicities, ages, and class. This cutting-edge series of novels, memoirs, and non-fiction writing welcomes the opportunity to present controversial views, explore multicultural ideas, encourage debate, and inspire creativity from a variety of lesbian perspectives. Through enlightening, illuminating, and provocative writing, Alice Street Editions can make a significant contribution to the visibility and accessibility of lesbian writing, and bring lesbian-focused writing to a wider audience. Recognizing our own desires and ideas in print is life sustaining, acknowledging the reality of who we are, our place in the world, individually and collectively.

Judith P. Stelboum
Editor-in-Chief
Alice Street Editions

Published by

Alice Street Editions, Harrington Park Press®, an imprint of The Haworth Press, Inc., 10 Alice Street, Binghamton, NY 13904-1580 USA (www.HaworthPress.com).

Portions of *The Thief's Journal*, by Jean Genet, ©1987, appear with kind permission of Grove/Atlantic, Inc.

Cover design by Thomas J. Mayshock Jr.

Cover Art by Alexandra Grilikhes: *Compass*. Box construction with found objects. *A box of artifacts, woven together with fragments of artifacts, suggests both the personal myth and the way in which the novel's elements have been traced, constructed, and woven.*

Library of Congress Cataloging-in-Publication Data

Grilikhes, Alexandra.
    Yin fire / Alexandra Grilikhes.
      p. cm.
    ISBN 1-56023-212-9 (alk. paper)–ISBN 1-56023-213-7 (pbk : alk. paper)
    I. Title.
PS3557 .R4899 Y56 2001
813'.54–dc21
                                                           2001022487

Yin Fire

Alexandra Grilikhes

Alice Street Editions

Harrington Park Press
New York · London · Oxford

for EMW

Acknowledgments

The author acknowledges, with gratitude, the extraordinarily dynamic and insightful presence of Charlotte Haines in the preparation of this book. Thanks also go to Phyllis Wachter and Carmella Viscuse for valuable commentary, to Michele Belluomini and Carol Coren for ongoing moral support, and to Karen Donnally for her perceptive and discerning friendship.

The author would like to acknowledge those magazines in which four chapters appeared as short fiction:

- "1503" in *Phoebe: An Interdisciplinary Journal of Feminist Scholarship, Theory and Aesthetics*. Fall, 1998.
- "The Letter" in *Fuel* 27/28, 2000.
- "Lovers, etc." in *The Brownstone Review*, Spring, 1999.
- "Mama: The Shrine" in *ART:MAG*, Spring, 1998.

Some of the material about Oriental medicine is based on the author's notes that were taken in courses given by Drew DiVittorio, Jeffrey Yuen and Denny Waxman.

CONTENTS

Venus in Scorpio

If she had been raised in the forest by wolves, Doris would have had a better idea of how to conduct herself in the world. As it was, she had been raised practically wild to not know what was expected of her by parents grieving the loss of their artistic selves, a brother absorbed in his burgeoning sexuality, a sister seized in the adolescent madness she would eventually overcome, but not until she forced Doris with her into her twisted vision of the world.

Doris had to learn every small and large thing there was to learn in the world on her body. And she can prove it by her scars. Her healed broken fingers, one on each hand. The scratched mosquito bite on her right forearm "frozen" by a doctor's medicinal spray before being sliced open and healed to scar. The dark blue (from the dark blue of her jeans) scars on both shins from a bad fall on the ice; the bit of black lead pencil point (palm center, right hand), the leg-shaving scar she tore off so many times it gave up trying to go away. Both broken toes. Her missing tooth, the largest in her mouth, lower right incisor. The way she learned was through her muscles and nerve endings; that way she remembered. If she tried to learn through reasoning or admonition or thinking it turned into an exercise in pain, futility, non-mastery.

Rooted deep in Doris's astrological chart was her Venus in Scorpio. Which meant difficulty in love. Too much emotion. Into the dark. She becomes molten lava and it has nothing to do with wanting or not wanting to be like that. She is where the planets point her on the date, the evening, the moment of her birth. Venus in Scorpio; first woman, first creature to know the place as water from which, wide and easy, the street flows.

It is a street she walks in her soul. A street which holds both secrets and answers—the wide girth of Gurney Street. But oh, to know the place from which she has set forth as if for the first time—where it is midnight, it will always be midnight—she will

1

never be free of it. It's wideness will never diminish, its face never dismantle. Even now she's driven to half-run down its wave of asphalt, looking, always looking for a certain thing, a key maybe.

She walks the wide girth of Gurney Street. As if she has been shot forth by the crash of the ocean which is separated from the street by a ten-foot-thick sea wall made of asphalt and cement.

But there is also that other street, Eleventh, between Fifth Avenue and Sixth, that other beginning place.

Cold.

Thick spit roils in her throat. She gathers it up, coughs unobtrusively, and delivers it to the dry mud at the base of a tree.

An ordinary tree-lined street in Greenwich Village. These are the woods of her past, the place from which she has set forth, the thick forest. Every week, winter and summer, she comes to this neighborhood to study Chinese Medicine and walk this street. On the next block is the building where her courses are given; her small school rents the space, Twelfth Street, fourth floor. She could easily go around this block, but every week she makes herself go down the path to shake herself up. Go down the path. Do it finally. Go in deep. Like sex. Today it is bitter cold. Cold sex.

Eleventh Street between Fifth and Sixth Avenues. Closer to Sixth. A place to which she returns. That won't leave her alone. She doesn't necessarily want to know the reasons. Just go there. Breathe into it. Let it come.

She turns her head to the right and finds herself looking into the windows of the ground floor apartment at 51 West, which is separated from the street by a thin wall of masonry and red brick.

The room seems brightly lit. Doris had once lived in this building for five years, and passed countless times through its inner and outer doors, crept up and down its six flights to her tiny apartment, which was dominated by the big desk whose stubby legs she sawed off so she could get it through the door, a job she did alone, kneeling on the floor in the hallway outside her door, thinking there was nothing she couldn't do in those days, mostly because there wasn't anyone around to ask for help.

Once sawed, the desk could fit through the door, but without legs it was so low that when she sat down her knees couldn't fit underneath it.

She had to lean all the way down to its surface in order to write or read; she wrote and read nonetheless. On a bitter January eve when the fuses blew, she lit twenty-eight candles on the surface of the desk so she could peer all night at the floor plans of medieval cathedrals for her comprehensive examination the next morning. She memorized them in that dim but not warming candlelight.

With her Venus in Scorpio, she'd lived and wept in this apartment building, sixth floor front, had shaken with anxiety, shaken with love, had felt imprisoned and ripped by love in this house, had looked suddenly in the mirror one day and asked, with dread in her voice, "Who are you?" She had looked out of the window hundreds, no, thousands of times, killed the same plant with neglect over and over on the windowsill, but she had never before seen this street-level apartment or known of its existence. Although she had not known the exact layout of each apartment, she thought she'd known pretty well every cranny of the building and its position on each of the six floors; yet now, suddenly, at this moment, a large box-shaped room lit-up at early evening, a ponderous diamond-shaped iron grate across both of its windows, was revealed to her.

Hawked-up spittle.

Gurney Street. That other place. The sea. This street its mirror.

Her feet hurtling down the street after her.

Jammed with furniture, the room is dimly if unevenly lit by a floor lamp standing in one corner. A woman is seated on the arm of a stuffed chair talking on the telephone in what appears to be the living room. At the instant the room flashes into her view and she sees the woman, Doris trips on a hole in the sidewalk and cracks her ankle so badly she cannot stand up for the pain.

It's as if a hole has opened and she is pulled into it by some incredible force. Thrown into the hole created when the opposing plates of the sidewalk don't meet. Where The Underworld bulges suddenly in her path just as she's gazing into the interior of a room at a woman she has never before seen instead of at the path in front of her.

In the room the woman is talking intently, the phone gripped in her hand, her eyes fastened on something not in the room. Doris's eye catches this momentary drama right before she spins down the crack towards The Underworld. To which she is overdue for a trip. A trip she has already set out for. A trip she is on. And the pain tells her as she makes several involuntary low moans and limps over to lean, then sit on a nearby step, that somewhere on this street something holds the key. That all she needs do is keep walking this street, tracking her way North or South. After X number of false starts, something will wake her up to who and what she is.

She understands that she is compelled here, knowing neither the reason nor the object of her search. But she is still bent on the search. It feels as if the key to The Underworld may be hidden somewhere on this street. What she needs is to keep tracking her way West or East until after the right number of missteps and fumblings, some magic will tell her who and what she is—a woman, lover of women, daughter of the Lady of the Beasts, the Mistress of the Animals, the bear-mother-hovering-woman-figure, the one she is forever seeking and loving or longing to love.

The bear/woman, Mistress of the Animals (called in ancient Greek the *Potnia Theron)* is a woman with many faces, none of which Doris has ever seen, because the woman is always surrounded by mist.

Although the Great Mother is the oldest of all of the deities the Mistress of the Animals is nearly as old. She is primitive and powerful. Doris knows her as the one who has mastery over the wild beasts that are both inside and outside of her. In early sculpture and paintings she is surrounded by animals, grasping a beast in each arm or hand. It is she who has power over Scorpions, she who can tame them, she who can teach Doris to mitigate the powerful dark side of Scorpio.

This woman, her Mother of Many Eons, is taller and bigger than Doris and doesn't know any of the names she is known by, or even who she is. Or that she is surrounded by a strange mist. But she is home to Doris. Home in the best and truest sense that there is no other person, place or thing that is home to her but this woman-figure she sometimes encounters, is enchanted by, this fairy godmother, the queen of her desires, the first object of her feelings, the beginning and the end of them. Doris is afraid of her also.

Doris names the Potnia Theron's adumbrations in the following people who have crossed her path: her second-grade teacher on whose nude body she crawled in her imagination, the two of them in a state of erotic bliss, the teacher a full-grown woman, Doris six years old.

Regina Brown, the English teacher; Lois Carter, who became a lawyer; Edwarde Weinstein, the head of the dance department; Portia Forrest of the counseling program; Gretel Lanker, the archaeologist; Hongwei Zhu, the Chinese doctor.

Larger in every way and more clumsy than Doris, Gretel Lanker was the possessor of arcane knowledge. Her native language was Dutch. She was shy, supremely reserved, aloof. Always embarrassed. With a rich voice, big face and large head, she was a hearty sort of athletic Earth Mother. Thick glasses. Blue eyes that looked watery behind her lenses. She was very proper acting, but the propriety seemed as if it was just for show.

Portia Forrest. Taller, heavier than even Gretel Lanker. Anglo-Saxon with pale blue eyes that were sort of fearful and frozen looking. A big Earth Mother, athletic, yet soft enough to relax into. Maybe. An unemotional voice, high and girlish. Heavy, wide shoulders. A squeaky undeveloped voice coming out of those huge chunky shoulders and big white womanly body. Body full of shame over itself. Drinking diet soda. Always trying to lose weight.

Edwarde Weinstein. Six feet two. Blue phoenix-shaped eyes, epicanthic-fold eyelids. Piercing eyes. So obviously a dyke. So big she displaced a lot of space. A sexy, lazy kind of voice. Not intellectual. Very unavailable. Loves to flirt.

All of the the others bore similarities to these except for Regina Brown who was short and powerful. Who sent Doris a postcard during one summer vacation that knocked her out. *I know now the awful fascination volcanoes have for the timid* was the cryptic message in blunt, blue ball-point script that had been pressed deep into the surface of the card. How could she know, Doris shivered, how could she articulate so well my deepest feelings? That she, her great intellect, her knowing manner, her beauty, is the volcano. Doris can't exactly recall but the photo might have been of the Grand Canyon. Or maybe it was just of trees, sky and grass.

The effect of each of these women on Doris—Dreaming awake. Speechlessness. Magnetized. Struck Dumb. Hot. Grabbed. Dazzled. Ablaze with longing. Obsession.

On that street a week later Doris slows her steps but doesn't dare stop. She looks closely at the place where the cement is broken. At the hole in the ground. The Underworld shows through today as a small muddy hole with a cigarette butt partly ground into the mud. Today it seems devoid of magic. Facing the broken cement is a window covered with an old metal diamond-shaped grate. Jammed inside the window, an ancient, beat-up air conditioner—a museum piece. Through the slats of the Venetian blinds she sees a straggly green plant atop the air-conditioner, the only life in the room. The room's ceiling light, dim against the early Manhattan dusk makes everything super-real. She passes the building and looks closely at the broken cement on the street and the shielded ground-floor windows. She is amazed at the glitter and puck of her imagination.

Only a week ago she'd tripped and fallen at this spot and been badly jerked into the painful memory of the women she had loved, all of them melting into an ancient mythical figure, the Mistress of the Animals, the Old One, second in age only to the Great Mother in the imagination of people since before time.

Doris, who recognizes the Mistress in so many places and guises, knows that the Mistress still manages to elude her.

Doris can see that nothing really changes except you. And although you change, you remain in your core, the Old One, the one you seek in others, the one lying in wait inside you. It was this truth that her fall in the street gave her.

Didn't everything Doris learned have to be learned on the body? She could barely walk. Limping down Eleventh Street towards Sixth, she prayed her ankle would hold her up. Prayed she'd be able to keep walking this path on her two feet. That she could keep moving and maybe find the key even if it meant she would have to stumble again and fall headlong downwards.

1503

Leaving the bookstore she let the heavy door shut behind her. She heard the woman's low voice. Any change? said the voice. She had walked twenty feet before she realized it was a woman's voice. She slipped off her glove, grasped the change purse from her right coat pocket, unzipped it and drew out three, no four quarters, walked back abruptly and dropped them into the paper cup at the woman's feet.

The woman, tall and black, was seated on a box. She nodded, even smiled, saying thank you as she looked carefully at the row of silver coins. Doris could see there had been exactly one nickel in the cup before her quarters had clunked in.

She hadn't been prepared for the feeling of electricity that rippled across her shoulders at the sound of the woman's voice. The sound of the thank you. Was it satisfaction? A burden lifted?

She could feel some difference in herself as she retraced her steps away from the woman. Cheaply bought, she thought, even as the feeling radiated through her body.

It was towards the end of January. She and her sister Solveig walked or rather meandered down 47th Street as if they had all the time in the world.

She had driven her blue Renault in from Princeton and found a legal parking spot. Only now did she recall the emptiness of the jewelry district in Manhattan on Saturdays. Of course.

She felt a combination of intensity and spaceyness, had felt it for weeks after Papa died. They had put off going to their father's office to gather his personal effects, but Doris knew the rent would be due the first of February. Solveig hadn't wanted to come. But Doris thought nineteen was old enough to take some responsibility, so she had asked and Solveig had given unenthusiastic assent.

8

They walked slowly down the street, their arms full of large manila envelopes. The envelopes contained papers and small objects they were taking with them. Tomorrow, their cousin Harald would come and remove the tools and small motor he wanted. He would pay their mother fifty dollars for the motor—a gesture more than anything, Doris knew.

Among the sketches and elegantly penciled diagrams of watch-cases and watchbands, the envelopes also held more of the girlie postcards she'd found hidden in Papa's closet at home.

Odalisques stretched out coquettishly on couches or chaises longues wearing only stockings and garters, some holding a fragile-seeming scarf in one hand. Their rouged cheeks and the bright orange, pink and blue of the couch pillows seemed un-touched by age.

Doris felt certain Solveig had never seen them. Never been as curious, perhaps, as she had been, scheming to steal the key to the locked bookcase from her mother's thick ring of keys so she could devour Flaubert or Pierre Loüys or the *Tales from Boccac-cio*, heart racing because her parents might come home early and catch her.

Years before that she had poked and sifted through Papa's closet shelf by shelf to try to discover his secrets. More than once she had found his postcards of naughtily flirting women tucked among his World War mementos—the wood handle of a rifle, a shallow metal helmet, a book of photographs of the Great War, boxes of odd-shaped metallic pieces, inlaid, beautifully designed metal door-plates on which names would now never be engraved; small statues and figurines collected from every place he had ever traveled. An ancient oil lamp made of copper.

Now, in his office for the first time, underneath stacks of stationery and envelopes and countless sketches for watchcases, they'd found pencil drawings of nude men and women.

On one sheet of paper, the man lay back, head resting on his folded arms, while a woman kneeled over him, holding his penis in her mouth with both hands. The man's eyes were closed. On another, a man and woman crouched over each other, their mouths on each others' genitals.

There were other drawings of women posing, by themselves or with other women. The drawings were unmistakeably his, his way of working the line on the page, his fine unmistakeable style.

She could see his face shadowed in the light of the living room as he carved his passionately spiraling designs into and through thick blocks of wood. She remembered the jeweler's loupe in his eye, intent on the infinitesimal workings of a watch. Now she had found the drawings and they repelled as much as they drew her. As she flipped through them, she paused, examining each of them.

Her sister turned away. They're not his, she said. Somebody gave them to him. Doris stopped herself from answering and watched as Solveig gathered the sheets of drawings and slid them into a manila envelope. The sketched pencil line was light, faded here and there, yet precise, too.

Her last glance around the room took in the battered saucepan, an old tablespoon, a stained hotplate. They looked as if they had been there forever. She had never before seen the strange tools, which must have been for engraving, but she picked out a few and put them into an envelope for herself.

They closed the door that had his name painted on the glass, next to the room number, 1503. The elevator seemed slow to arrive and even slower to get to the first floor. As they left the building, Doris wanted to pull the envelope out of Solveig's hands so she could take it home and pore over the drawings for as long as she wanted. She had to see on paper, under the light, what that part of him was about.

When she was twelve, he had crawled into her bed and cupped his hand over her breast, the four-year-old Solveig soundly asleep in the other bed. Her mother away at a PTA meeting, he had come in, he said, to kiss her goodnight. For years before that he'd stroked her thighs, stroked her upper arms, especially the underneath part, which gave her feelings of pleasure and fear. When no one else was around, her big brother had done exactly the same things to her. She had always pretended that nothing was happening; she hadn't known what else to do. Now her father was dead, and she and Solveig had found the drawings and postcards he had hidden in his office. This was the part about him she hadn't been able to confide to anyone. The part of him that said, go ahead, kick your feet in the water I won't drop you and then dropped her, saying see, you're swimming. But she wasn't.

They walked in the direction of her car from 48th to 47th Street. Suddenly Solveig stopped before a group of trash cans and tipped the envelope with the drawings into the trash. It was gone in an instant. Solveig did not speak, and, after an intake of breath and surprised silence, neither did Doris.

The Deli stretched long and darkish before them; they were its only customers in mid-afternoon. They ordered coffee for themselves, and hardly spoke in the quiet. One side of the booth was mirrored, but they did not look in the mirror. Each of the tables held a stainless steel bowl filled with pickled green tomatoes and cucumber pickles. The bowls were covered with divided metal lids that could be opened either on one side or the other.

Solveig began devouring first a tomato, then several pickles, her teeth crunching rapidly on the flesh. The juice ran down the table into her napkin and saucer. Doris tasted a tomato. It was as sour as anything she had ever tasted and she put it into a corner of her napkin and rolled up the napkin. She pushed her saucer and spoon around on the table with small movements for awhile, then they got up and left. She wanted to shake Solveig by the shoulders and shout at her, *Why did you do that, you had no right!* The drawings didn't fit Solveig's picture of their father, but for Doris they fit; they fit just right.

The Letter

Sometimes, I don't know why, I have trouble breathing. As if my breath is passing me by, has gone somewhere else. Someone else is breathing me.

I make a short train trip to meet you halfway, so we can travel to New York together in your car for a couple of hours. You present me with a box of seashells that you've found on a beach in Miami on one of your trips. Some of them are cracked and broken. I don't have the energy to say I don't want them. If I take them I won't be able to just toss them. They belong to the sea so I'll have to make a trip to the ocean to give them back. Annoyed at my inability to say no, I take the box and lay it on top of, not inside, the bag that rests on my lap. Another burden. An expressionless thank you falls from my mouth.

You're pleased to think I've accepted your gift so promptly. You don't know what kind of shells I like and you don't bother to ask. You think I should be grateful for your shells.

Seatbelt fastened tight, you drive in your purposeful way, after I've refused to fasten mine. Then it will be *your* responsibility you offer pompously. That's right, I agree.

Occasionally, I look over at the map you have spread out, and comment on the route you've chosen. It would be rude to doze my way through this trip, though that's what I'd like. Since it's our only chance to visit this year, I make the effort to chat, allude to our friendship, but I no longer trust you. I know you've dissected me behind my back with my lover. You don't know that I know.

I'm aware also that every word I say is being memorized by you to be written in your journal, verbatim.

This makes me weigh every word and consider what I want to have recorded forever—sentence, comma, pause—in your precise spidery script.

I stick to desultory chatter.

12

You don't know how I've come to despise you, though perhaps you're beginning to wonder at how impersonal I've become. Colder. Not asking advice as I usually do after you've said, how are things with B.? Because you've betrayed our friendship.

I still, however, owe you $2000 on the loan. It creates an artificial bond between us.

When I think of the charming gifts you send at Christmas or Valentine's Day—a vase from Chinatown, a cloth heart that opens into small red rooms, a carved green moon overlayed with your designs and carefully traced inscriptions, I can't believe how beautiful they are. I shake my head.

No one has ever written me such love letters. My lover rarely talks of love, only money, which is her sole passion. Last year, when I hesitatingly mentioned to her a searing love letter I'd written a few months earlier, she had said, incredulous, "You sent me a letter? What was it about?" A few days later while she was in the shower I had no trouble finding it among a jumble of papers in her drawer. I took it back and never mentioned it again.

But you whom I once loved like a sister I now hate.

I keep your letters; I know I'll never be lucky enough to receive anything like them again. I know how life is. You can find yourself with an uncommunicative lump for reasons you don't understand. In my daybook I write my lover a letter I'll never send; "You don't know how to love." But three years earlier I'd written the exact words to my previous lover. What a shock to find word for word the same entries in my earlier diaries. What are you doing to yourself I say, shutting the book quick.

Sitting beside you, driving the jail-drab Belt Parkway, I imagine your fantasy: We are lovers on a trip together, your old dream. The reality is that, at your suggestion (our only face-to-face meeting this year), while driving home to Maine from a trip to Florida, you are giving me a ride to Queens where I am going to see my mother who is eighty-seven and half-blind. She has a cast on her right arm; her wrist is broken in three places from a fall out of bed.

When I arrive, I help Esme, the homecare attendant, undress and wash her.

"Look at these breasts. Did you know I nursed all four of my children?" she says. "All of them." I put a small amount of moisturizing lotion under the folds of her breasts as Esme directs me. I do it awkwardly. Her body is still Mama but she feels strange to me. Her boniness. She points to her pubic hair. "Look, it isn't gray, it's fair." I look because she wants me to see her as she is. What she has become is frightening. We wash her as much as she will allow with a washcloth and warm water.

"I've had four children," she says, pointing to her belly. "Would you ever have guessed?" "No," we both say. "Never," I add.

You have no trouble refusing gifts. Driving along in grim silence, the shells in their plastic container that is still half in and half out of my bag, how I'd love to assert (as you so easily would) "Thank you no. They're not the kind I like." But I've been so distant I feel I should break the tension a little and try to soften this hard trip.

Your letters.

I remember the summer we become friends. I manage to find myself two free months at the resort where you live and I spend them painting. We meet almost daily and we talk easily. On the day before going home I say goodbye and kiss you lightly on the cheek. I don't want to be your lover, never want it. Although you have a lover at the time, I find your note tacked to my door—done in your characteristic style—a postcard with a stunning photo on one side. "Your kiss was the star in my sky," written on the other side in your blackest ink.

We discover that we grew up on the same street in the Bronx, and that neither of us has traveled back there after we have left for good. You come into my life precisely at the moment when I need a guide to walk back with me over that bridge to take pictures of the streets as they are now. Still home, of course, but not home, never again home. The streets of both of our childhoods: cars parked that will never start again, houses burned down or boarded up. You are the guide who will lead me back over the dangerous passes to that precipice from which I jumped early—home. When we meet, we each think of traveling back there together; we are eager to make the trip. There is no one else with whom either of us can do this.

One bitter cold February weekend we travel by subway, then slowly, painfully make our way over the bridge on foot. As we walk I urge you to hide the camera you have hanging around your neck by its strap but you say "I refuse to live like a dog," and, to my amazement, nobody bothers us.

I feel blasted out by this desolate trip to my childhood, but your presence makes it something more; a voyage to a strangely familiar alien island. And a ritual.

I sleep on the only bed of the borrowed Lower East Side apartment, while you sleep on the floor because I'm unable to sleep in the bed with you in it. You don't mind. You are smiling and softly humming. This weekend you seem happier than I've ever seen you. "I'm never hungry when I feel like this; I don't need ordinary things like food," you declare when I want to stop to get something to eat. All you want is coffee.

In a few days you send me an oversize postcard, which hangs on my wall for years, a magnificent reproduction of a half-nude sculpted goddess from Rajasthan, 9th or 10th century, permanent collection, the Brooklyn Museum. On the other side, an exquisite love letter from you.

I walked home and the city was beautiful, so clear & with buildings lit up at Madison Square w/their windows reflecting the deep silvery blue of dusk; oh & walked East on 17th Street from Union Square, some fine old buildings & one low house w/8 ' high windows, lights on, huge plants climbing inside in pots, and a piano sonata on the phonograph. It was all so filling, so beautiful, & I gave some change to an old black man who says he's been in AA for 8 months now, all but 4 who went into detox with him are in jail or dead now, he doesn't go in bars any more but goes to movies & church and just enjoys life.—it was so beautiful & I know it was just my happiness, I haven't felt so radiant and right in a long time, it's become an unaccustomed state: I love being with you. I guess you know that. I was too shy to tell you about the fantasy I had some time ago, maybe november, of walking across the bridge with you hand-in-hand like children: and then to stand in the courtyard of 1501—Teddy the nice black man used to paint the courtyard entrance cement a dull red every year—and kiss deeply, yes, you & I. I felt in some way that that would restore the balance, that it would mean the social acceptance by the world of my childhood (i.e., the world that taught me the rules and morality & how society works) a kind of retrospective blessing of me as a person by the powers that were in that childhood world, when the neighborhood is all the world & adults the real gods. There was also the resonance of that fantasy of a sacrament, the kiss in sacred environs, a holy space, as kind of marriage sacrament. (So I ask you, who's crazier? No, I know myself utterly sane). And I love you.

As a postscript, you add *But perhaps this is premature, an exaggeration.*

The postcard itself, with its voluptuous sculpture on the front, is beautiful, but your construction is more a work of art than a real letter. At least that's what I allow myself to think. Because I can never love you I am doubly moved by your words. They seem distant and elegant like literature, though kind of "gone," and from a stunningly beautiful place I have visited only briefly.

Besides, you are the one I think of as my friend, my guide.

Two years earlier, during a vacation visit B. and I make to Maine, you and B. have brunch together at a seaside restaurant while I prowl the beach, scavenging beachglass, and, all that summer, small, flesh-colored stones. A few days later I find your diary in your bedside drawer—you are almost never without it—and while B. is outside smoking and you are at work, I flip to the date of the brunch and find the dialogue exactly inscribed in your neat hand.

B. says that Doris is just like Doris's mother. She can't stand to be alone. If you want to know what someone's really like, look at the mother I always say! B. confides that she and her ex-lover, M., live really well together at B.'s house, have the same sort of sheet- and towel-folding habits. You must tell Doris that! I warn her. That you are comfortable with your living arrrangements and that she'll just have to get used to them.

I pore over the finepointed script, my heart and pulses pounding. Read swiftly the exact dialogue between you: B's complaints about me and your advice. I copy with shaking hands—lest B. come in and find me—onto the end papers of the book I happen to have with me—*The Selected Plays of Antonin Artaud*—pages I rip out and stash god knows where. Speedwriting because I must know exactly what B. is confiding as you eagerly invite. How you advise her to deal with me. I copy every word.

After that summer, the next time you come to visit, I pretend that nothing has changed though I'm furious at your betrayal, your switching of friendships. You, of course, behave like my solicitous trustworthy friend. Your parting gift to me this trip is a rare oblong beach stone four inches long, which becomes the surface on which I find myself fiercely incising with a blueblack ballpoint pen, over and over around the outside edges the words:

DIE BITCH DIE.

I stash the stone somewhere—anywhere—as long as I don't have to look at it. Sometimes when I uncover it accidentally—although it is hidden, I never know when it will turn up among my things—I am struck, no, made breathless by the wild energy I see in the acid-shaped letters I've so deeply incised. The energy of my passion is palpable, overwhelming. I find myself modifying the words one day because I realize that I'm seriously wishing you dead. Gripping the pen I print **IN MY HEART   IN MY TRUST IN MY FRIENDSHIP   AS MY GUIDE** around the edges of the stone. Small mitigation.

I never want to let you know that I know about your perfidy.
How now you are her friend in whom she confides while you let
me think you are still my confidante. Not letting on that you take
her part against mine, advising her how to deal with me so that
she can remain in control. You know how to do this. You are
good at it. Then you write everything in your spidery script, leaving
out not so much as a breath. And every word a judgement.

Propelled forward in the beat-up prison of your car, I can feel
you imagining us a couple taking a trip together, your fondest
dream. I know the impossibility of the fantasy but also how
wonderful it has been to receive your letters. You are probably
furious with me for being unable to feel what you want.

You keep whatever you feel inside.

A truck has broken down ahead of us and traffic is barely
inching along. After thirty minutes, I keep looking at my watch.

Everything in your car is carefully organized, every mile clocked,
how much gas you've used.

Calculated.

The map opened right. You ask me to fold the map of New
Jersey because now we are in New York. Fold it the right way,
you order. The excessiveness of your intellectual life, the giving of
too many directions are what make me feel like I can't breathe.
Yes, my lover is prosaic, unromantic. Secretive. Sometimes tongue-
tied. Aside from the subject of money, all she talks about are her
dogs, Spike and Lulu; she has no artistic or intellectual life

But her ways are mysterious to me. "I'd like to become rich and
famous," she announces one day, free, for a moment, of her
preoccupation with mortgages, stocks and bonds, columns of
numbers. Always adding columns, she complains of headaches and
falls asleep in my bed, no energy left for love. But wanting me
there.

But you. You're mysterious in a dull way. When I take your
picture to the psychic she says, "There's some important part
missing from this person."

When the psychic looks at my lover's photo, she hesitates. "See how the whites of her eyes are visible on either side of, and below the pupils? I'd be very careful."

"What do you mean," I mutter, my voice so low I hear it as a hum when I listen to the tape later, "about the whites of the eyes?"

"That," she whispers, "shows instability. When you see the whites of their eyes like that. Instability. Usually all of their lives. Unless," she pauses, "once in a great while, you might find someone who is able to change as a result of being loved a great deal. But it's rare," she whispers,"very rare."

If I could have fallen in love with letters I would have chosen you, but the you that I know is remote from your letters. Can you really have written them?

My mother's tiny body is wrapped in clean pajamas, her unruly hair cut and let fall to the floor in a white heap, on spread newspapers, then vacuumed up. Esme marvels, "Look how thick, how alive her hair is! So thick, so alive!" I think, what a body will become.

I feel the pressure of your company and of the guarded self I have to be with you, watching every word I say. A pity.

"We'll be there soon," I venture. You ask me if I have a check for you on the loan. "Oh yes," I answer, taking it out and sliding it into your wallet compartment as you crisply direct me.

You expand on your travels. "For two months I've never been lonely, not even once. On this trip I've driven alone, looked at everything on the streets, gone to every museum in every town and county. I have all the catalogs." I make the "mmmm" sound that allows me to pretend neither approval nor disapproval.

What's the use, I think, of looking in every piddling museum when you don't know how to be my friend any more. Or lover either. You think knowledge is waiting for you in museums. They give you a purpose.

I pay for the tolls, but you won't let me pay for the gas.

You pull up near the apartment building where my mother lives and I turn to get out and say goodbye. And to thank you.

"Do you think you might come north this summer?" You sound, for a moment, less crisp.

"It's possible," I answer, in a hearty tone. You drive off, your map neatly before you, your mile chart at your side.

My mother, who doesn't know one day from the next, is neither prepared nor unprepared for my arrival. The scissors I've borrowed from my lover to cut my mother's hair lie in my bag under the box of seashells. In order to get out of your car, I have to twist myself awkwardly out of the seat, and at the same time push the shells deep into the bag. They'll stay there for a long time.

Gurney Street

It is you whom I think about and picture. Even now.

I walk the wide girth of Gurney Street towards the ocean whose high waves I can hear smashing against the shore.

It is nearly midnight.

Jordan and I are headed towards Gloria's, a bar that becomes gay after midnight. Someone has told us this. But you have to be careful cruising. Although it is also a straight bar, it's the only place for gay people to go in this small beach town. We've come for a weekend. We are both a little dressed up, but casual. We're staying in the Seacrest, a guest house owned by a highly visible but closeted dyke, Harriet O'Toole. We have adjoining rooms on the second floor. We are best friends. The bath is in the hall but at least my room has a sink in one corner. It is a hot, airless, but adequate room. Jordan wants to meet guys or maybe a guy. I want to meet women or maybe a woman. We're both nervous but we have different kinds of fear.

Jordan and I enter Gloria's. It is large and dark with a huge horseshoe shaped bar and a big, noisy jukebox. We stand and chat a little self-consciously, trying to appear sophisticated by comparison to the small-town people standing around us, all trying to look as if they are perfectly at home.

We sit at the bar and sip our drinks, murmuring about someone's face or hairstyle, covertly cruising, despite the fact that we look like a straight couple. We have begun to see some people who might be gay—a few nondescript men seem to suddenly appear. A solid young black guy who seems to know them all chats vociferously. Nobody seems swishy,

Jordan recognizes Chet, a boyish guy who's cruised him on the boardwalk. He thinks Chet looks like a hairdresser—too faggy and his bleached hair has an orange cast. But he talks to Chet because Chet knows the scene. A young woman appears among them, talking and laughing. I notice her out of the corner of my eye, but ignore her, slowly sipping my drink, and looking at the people opposite me. I can't tell a thing about anyone. Through Chet, Jordan has been introduced to a few of the men; he comes over and sits with me for a while to tell me sotto voce that they seem to be gay but that he's not interested. He indicates this by closing his eyes and giving his head a few small shakes like he's in pain. God, he says. He is a slender man in his late twenties with a thick brown mustache and sad brown eyes. Under cover of animated chatter he makes fun of them as being flitty, or dumb. He turns his attention to a man sitting opposite us who he says resembles Howdy Doody because of his bangs and funny hairstyle. The man is soon joined by a woman much taller and heavier than he. She is weighed down by a hefty leather pocketbook with thick straps. They appear ill at ease, their eyes dart around the room. They barely converse, nor do they once look at each other. The man is tiny, but very handsome and built like a weightlifter. I decide they are both gay and married to each other for cover in this small New Jersey town, and that he lifts weights in his spare time to make up with muscle what he lacks in height. Like us, they have come to cruise.

Years later I find out he is attracted to boys in their teens and married to her for cover. That she is straight. Or maybe never discovered what she is.

I decide, after a few cursory looks, that she is a nurse who has just come from the night shift to meet him for a drink, an agreed-upon ritual. They have nothing to say to each other although they are roommates. She doesn't stay for long. He continues, very nervously, to cruise after she leaves.

I observe her with curiosity because she reminds me of Alice, my first lover, the heavy-set older woman I had come out with—her thirty-two years to my nineteen. For a year I had been addicted to the power she had over me. Just her gaze, long and deep into my eyes, or her talking to me in her seductive voice, or, for that matter, any voice, was enough to make me wet. But one day when she asked "Would you want to live with me?" my eyes grew wide and I hesitated without answering just long enough to hear her say, "forget it" and laugh. She had caught me in my deceit; I didn't really like her. There is nothing we can talk about. I am just interested in the experience of sex with her, sex and its surround; the excitement, the affair.

I have read everything I can lay my hands on about sex—gay sex, lesbian sex. Anything—novels, biographies, even Krafft Ebing's *Psychopathia Sexualis.*

When she finally borrows a friend's apartment on the Upper West Side one rainy afternoon, I am eager, though very nervous. I discover that her idea of sex is that we kiss and stroke each other. Then when she feels we are sufficiently aroused we are to each masturbate and try to come at the same time. Something in me refuses to do this. So I lie there listening to her breath quicken until she comes. When she realizes she's doing it alone, she thinks I'm just shy, that I'll become more relaxed with the idea when we know each other better. But I don't want a second time. I don't understand, at first, that she needs me there while she masturbates, that that is sex to her. I feel cheated by her desire for her own flesh.

All this goes rapidly through my mind as I glance at the thickset, dark woman gulping her drink in the bar, making an appearance with her gay husband to give him the straight exterior he needs in this tiny beach town. She isn't really gay, he is, I think. A gay woman would never come to cruise in her hometown bar wearing a business suit and carrying a giant purse. It isn't sophisticated.

Three hours later, neither of us has found anyone who attracts us. Jordan and I make our way home to the Seacrest after three A.M., feeling as though we've inexplicably missed out on some adventure. As if what we have just experienced can't be all there is of gay life in Causeway. Walking the silent, deserted pavements of Gurney Street, we trail our way home. A few hours hence, we will be awakened by the loud singing of hymns from inside the church that is catercorner to the guest house.

Chatting and laughing with false gaiety, we are relieved; neither of us has found anyone even mildly interesting. We are gossiping about the boys we've seen, and the girl I finally talked to.

"What do you do?" she'd asked me.

Sizing her up as a college student—too callow for me—pleasantly androgynous, but with no breasts and that was not good enough, I'd answered, just out of the blue, "I'm a microbiologist."

"Oh," she said, "where?"

"I hate talking about work when I'm not working," I'd answered, to end that part of the conversation. I want someone with a little mystery I think. A woman.

At this point, the idea of picking someone up in a bar is a lot more attractive to me than actually doing it. I play at it but don't do the real thing until much later, unlike Jordan who frequently goes home with tricks he picks up in bars. I've got to go out Saturday night, he'll say. I have to get rid of it. Rid of what, I think, disdainful. Is that what sex is to you? Getting rid of something? But I don't say it aloud.

The choreography of cruising. How Chet can be searching Jordan's eyes and face with such intensity you'd swear he was madly in love with Jordan instead of just wanting Jordan to fuck him in the ass or maybe to give Jordan a blow job. Or both. And then go on to the next guy.

That sudden desire, that play acting of passion is compelling for me. So symbolic, so immediate, so hot. And so ridiculous. It seems to me though, like the substance of life. It seems real.

The next weekend we arrive at Gloria's an hour before midnight, excited all over again. This time a live band is playing good music, and we dance all night to Joe Cocker's "Doin' All Right." Its syncopation makes me forget my actual dread of meeting someone who could get to me. Someone who might know me better than I know myself. Someone who could exercise power over me. Someone I can't control. Excited. Yet we knew that probably nothing would happen. Nothing happening meant no sex. When someone says "Maybe something will happen," or "Did anything happen?" it is a question about sex. "Something" or "anything" seems always to mean sex, but it is called "anything happening."

It isn't by lust we are drawn but by the need to find other people like us, to just be around them for comfort. I decide to spend my three-week-vacation at the Seacrest in August. I rent the efficiency apartment on the first floor for three hundred dollars. Jordan and I will see each other only on the weekends he comes to Causeway. I think I'll feel lost at Gloria's without him, so I decide not to go back until he's with me.

I have not yet met you, so I can't visualize you in your third-floor bedroom, a room filled with the worldly possessions you've moved here from New York in early spring. You keep Tiny, your beloved wirehaired terrier, in your room all day while you work at the gift and card shop owned by Harriet called Harrie's Gifts, taking Tiny for walks late at night, after you get home. If you remember. The room smells strongly of dogshit. You are most likely buzzed out drunk in your room in the Seacrest's back wing high above Harriet's kitchen where I haven't yet ventured. Or you might be smoking dope to calm yourself down after having worked your ten- to twelve-hour shift at the shop. I find out that you get room and board in exchange for working your ass off for her, but not much else.

A cigarette in one hand, a beer in the other, you might be sitting and waiting for Harriet to pay you a visit for quick sex. I won't find out till much later that you and she have been having an affair all summer. Toni, Harriet's lover of ten years, knows but pretends not to know so as not to make waves. She has nowhere else to go. She isn't actually Harriet's business partner, in spite of the fact that people frequently call her that. Like you, she works for Harriet, although unlike you, she has a place in Harriet's king-size bed at night. Since you're five feet tall and Harriet six, it's hard to imagine the two of you together in any position. I try not to think about it.

One Sunday evening I walk back through the house into the kitchen looking for Harriet in order to pay my bill for the weekend and find you sitting alone in the kitchen, smoking a cigarette. Your easy smile seems about to appear.

"I'm Doris Mills," I introduce myself.

"Lou Chatelaine," you offer back. "My real name's Eloise, but nobody's called me that since I was three."

"Chatelaine. Isn't that a French-Canadian name?" I want to know.

"No. As far as I know it isn't," you smile very pleasantly. "My family is Pennsylvania Dutch all the way back."

I am drawn to you. Is it boredom? Loneliness? All or none? I don't care. You are my height, small boned, fair. You smoke one cigarette after another.

I remain there, chatting about the origin of your name, though it's nearly departure time for my train. My subtext, however, is you, and we both know this.

During the first two weeks of my stay, since your room is at the back and mine at the front, and the house has double staircases, we never run into each other. Except one day I come out of my room at the moment you are descending the steps. We are face to face and I quickly tell you that I'm staying for three weeks in the efficiency and ask how you are doing and how you've been as if we are more than the merest of acquaintances.

"Thank you, I'm O.K., I'm O.K." You pause. "I just found out that my mother has cancer of the liver." You say you're concerned except that you don't use the word concerned; you make it sound like it's nothing serious. Nothing for anyone to be upset over.

"I called today and got the report from the doctor. I wasn't ready to hear that," you declare; "I wasn't ready at all." But you are almost smiling. I want to think it's serious, you are practically telling me she is dying, but your tone remains pleasant

"I'm sorry to hear it," I say, but I don't really know what to say. Something in you is telling me to not feel sorry for you, to not say too much. We end up muttering a few pleasantries and going our ways. You are unlike anyone I know; the subtext is something more, something we sense about each other that we both want to get close to. Need to.

The next time we see each other, Nixon is giving his Watergate address, and you, Harriet, Toni and all the guests are gathered in front of the television set in the living room. I come in and pretend to be interested in Nixon, but the back of your denim jacket with its circle of studs fascinates me. In my mind it is sexual, a sexual symbol, sort of the way a bull's-eye is. Like either you get it right or you don't, it being the right aim, the right touch, the right place, the right energy. The right combustion. Something I want very badly. Somehow I see it in that circle of studs.

I find out from you later that it was just a jacket, with no special meaning, and that you are sexually inexperienced. None of that matters. The chase, subtle and hidden, has begun.

One afternoon I'm sitting alone on the front porch, reading, and you appear with your large watering can for the plants on the porch to tell me the news that Harriet's mother has just passed away and that Harriet and Toni have left for the big family funeral in Delaware. You are in charge of the guest house in their absence. I understand immediately that our paths are meant to converge further, that Harriet's absence, plus the fact that it's Monday, means we'll be alone in the house for four days until the weekend guests begin to arrive. We are free I think, exultant. But you have an endless round of chores ahead of you, and, to my amazement, you do them all in order. I ask if you mind if I keep you company, or if you'd like my help. Very sweetly you say, "No, not at all." On the surface, your manner is to be sweet, always, I discover. In a week's time my vacation will be over.

Tonight you will have to do the laundry for all the rooms, tomorrow morning put clean sheets on every bed. You will be working practically the whole night. For the next twelve hours I do not leave your side. I sit opposite you in the kitchen next to the thrum of the washing machine and dryer and we tell each other the details of our lives. Of course only what we want the other to know at the moment. I help you to fold the sheets finally; you are a perfectionist in this, something I'm not at all good at. I'm impatient and anxious but now you control everything having to do with time; you are in charge of whatever is going to happen and maddeningly ritualistic about each of your tasks.

It is nearly two A.M. and I have helped you fold the last bath towel. There is a deep pause. Suddenly and slowly I place my right hand on your left shoulder, my palm curved on the curve of your shoulder. I have wanted to touch you all evening. You look back at me intensely, your questions unspoken. We say nothing to break the silence. The tension is almost unbearable. We climb the stairs to your room in the empty house. It is dark, delicious, secret, deserted. We fall onto the bed, exhausted, lightheaded. We are the same size, we fit together perfectly. While we are making love, Tiny quietly goes about chewing every button off the denim shirt I've thrown on the chair with the rest of my clothes.

When you open your eyes the next morning the first thing you do is take a couple of long swigs from a half-empty bottle of beer you have on your bedside table. I don't say anything because the only thing I seem to care about is bonding with you before Harriet gets home. She will want you back.

But by the time she arrives, we have made love in every bedroom where the sheets needed to be changed, while we were making the beds. We will never forget room numbers five and seven.

You are mine.

It is our first Saturday night. You know some gay guys who are giving a party on the other side of town across the street from the ocean and you are invited. Your friend Maria, who is staying at the Seacrest this weekend, drives us there. After the emotional drag of new love, sleepless nights and very little food, neither of us could have made it on our own.

At the party, the boys are in various stages of drunkenness. They're gesticulating and telling funny stories. You and I are the only women. They like you. They address you as "you cute little whippet you." They ignore me pointedly. I feel myself growing angrier by the moment. "Let's get out of here," I whisper urgently. You're pretty drunk—I've discovered you usually are by this time of night—but you're willing to leave with me despite the fact that these fellows shower you with attention because you look like a cute little boy—a type I have always found attractive. Gay men love you and feel comfortable with you. They see me as a woman who is, somehow, too serious.

Leaving the party, we find ourselves walking north, and suddenly decide to sit on the steep stone steps of 813 Beach, a narrow three-story Victorian. It is past midnight and very peaceful. We have been lovers for only a few days. Close to you or not, I can still feel the sensation of the hot flush of your body and your pulses racing close to the surface of your skin. We have passionately mixed our sweat, saliva, skin and bodies, yet we are strangers. Your scent is a combination of alcohol and tobacco with a tinge of sadness. Your essence, your wounds—all that ineffable stuff—combining perfectly with mine, dives into my heart and burrows. Below the surface we're communing in some secret way that seems fated. Even though I've spent years mucking around with my own destiny, trying to change it, none of that seems to matter now.

Still angry over what happened at the party, I lecture you on Women's Liberation and male privilege and how much I hate to be put down, ignored or dissed by men, gay or straight. I repeat this in several different ways and you agree, of course, to everything I say. You slur your words and speak with drunken vehemence. We're sitting on someone's stone steps in late summer, hot with desire and your face shines with sweat from the heat though it's one a.m. and breezy.

I can feel your body's luminous heat, and every time I touch even your arm, your fire. You vibrate, your hands tremble. You're drunk. You come from a small town. You're slender. Your eyes are green-blue. You look like a little boy and I'm nearly delirious. My pulses fast and loud, I feel tied in somebody else's knot, somebody else's bow.

My anger isn't spent but I'm wasting my breath because you will agree with anything I say. We kiss lightly not caring if anyone sees us. The feeling is unbelievably erotic; we kiss once more.

My heart's pounding nearly out of my chest. A few days later—or is it weeks—placing one hand on your chest, the other on my arm you will say, "My heart is pounding," and I won't be able to answer in words.

When she returns, Harriet understands right away that everything in her world at the Seacrest has been altered. Toni is secretly joyful; I can feel it.

Labor Day, which will be the day after tomorrow, is the last day of my vacation. You and I, still strangers, and still almost totally in the dark, will be at the beginning.

Lovers, etc.

Ship oars he said, sliding both oars back through his hands so that they clattered into the oarlocks. This is the way it's done.

The first breath. SAVASANA (Corpse Pose)

A dry leaf.
A dry leaf floating. On the water.
Rowing alone. A rowboat on Lake Farfara, the shore full of trees and punks. Marshy.
The oars in my hands. This is the way to ship oars, he said.
Feet bare. Bottom of the boat wet. Bottom of the boat wood. With the right oar dip fast into water over and over, the boat flips vertically, spins you around, nearly upends you in a medicine wheel. Sound of wood; water.
If you have a tendency to fall asleep during Savasana, try bringing your feet closer together.
You aren't asleep, you aren't awake. You feel tied in someone's knot, someone's bow. *Someone else.*
The darning needle in the wet bright air past your brow. It is June.
Oh Mother
Oh Father
I'm afloat in the world my arms, my legs. A dry leaf on the water. Floating.

My best lover, BHUJAN ASANA (Cobra Pose)

Twice my size, an Amazon, big and blonde. Her thighs and the rest of her, on the thick side. Small rosy mouth, tiny pug nose, curls that fell carelessly but always looked just right.

31

Kilts would have looked good on her. Lois.

During some of our stolen hours, her Volkswagen broke down in the middle of the Manhattan rush hour. Both of us crouched in the street to look at the flat tire, she, unconscious of those blond curls of hers, that little mouth, that butch-husky voice. A gorgeous Anglo-Saxon androgyne. Archetypal.

But never an interesting thought. Or, for that matter, a thought. She was a dumbbell who waited for you to offer one so she could respond. Her fingers were long and thick. She could make me come in three minutes with those fingers and a little tongue. I was able to fool Remi for an entire winter until she and I moved to Baltimore for Remi's new job. Lois stayed in New York and went to Law School. Throughout the vivid months of our affair, I swore to Lois that I would leave Remi for her, it was just a matter of time, and I thought I meant it at least some of the time. Fabulous sex or a jailer lover, what was the choice? That height, that moment of total orgasm could never again be approached in this life; she had no idea how fantastic a lover she was. It was the kind of thing you wouldn't want to tell, it would give the other person too much power over you, it was like that.

Whenever her ex-lover, who was also her roommate, was going to be home for dinner, Lois would eagerly announce, "I'm going to get fed tonight," making herself sound like a pet or a baby. Saying that, she'd chuckle, whether from shame or because she thought it was cute, I couldn't tell. How I despised her passivity, her dumbness, but how I wanted to experience that body. I was vile, ruthless, infatuated. Why is it that I still beat myself up for that little bit of unalloyed pleasure? Why is it that I still care? Yes, I was lying to two people just to get those few moments of beauty and truth flowing into my body to blast out through the crown of my head. That extreme pleasure, that once-in-a-lifetime experience; wholly giving myself to a dullard who knew what to do with me in spite of herself and her dullness.

I was 27.

That karma was going to come back to me in spades.

ARDHA-SALABHASANA (Half-Locust Pose)

After my neck injury and the enforced rest of almost a year made my muscles too weak to hold me up, my back went out and I could hardly walk. It was months of being on sick leave from work, waiting for my back to heal, and brooding. I was that lonesome and desperate for warmth, a body, someone to touch me, that I let Anna seduce me.

She was half my size, her voice high and whiney. The morning after the only night I let her stay over, I woke up, hung over from a tranquilizer sleep, to find her neatly showered, dressed and coiffed, lying across from me, writing busily in her journal, a small smile flickering across her lips, a smile of triumph. In her detached way, she'd managed the night before to make me come through sheer dogged patience. Her smile with its air of detachment was infuriating to see the first thing in the morning. It was as if she thought that exercising such power over me would forever place me in her control. I silently vowed never to sleep with her again just at the time when she thought our relationship was off to a flying start. I avoided her; I didn't return her phone calls; I answered her in monosyllables whenever we spoke in person. I let it show how exasperated I was to find her waiting outside the door to my apartment as often as I did.

It seemed to take forever for her to understand that my interest had become disinterest, dislike, even hatred.

Stephanie was much younger than me, tall and lanky, with smooth Anglo-Saxon features. She came from a family of very rich drunkards all of whom had tastes she regarded as undeveloped. Although Stephanie had gone to a fancy women's college, her idea of cultural depth was a concert by Melissa Manchester, something I disdained. Her first lover and former teacher, a woman much older than she, was dying of cancer. For some reason, whenever Stephanie spoke or happened to swallow, there was an audible gulp. She loved to tell stories about how she was desired by everyone who saw her—the electrician, lesbians, the bartender, the meter-reader. Talking about sex, she thought there had to be more to it than what she experienced with Susan, her lover, but she didn't know what. "Is that all there is to it," she would ask afterwards; "isn't there anything else?" Mealy, lifeless hands, a good tongue but thin in the soul. Her mouth was always dry. She licked her lips all the time to moisten them. My desire for her was from a hunger neither of us could assuage.

At night, the only way I could fall asleep was with the help of sleeping pills and a tall glass of sherry. An orthopedic surgeon had given me a set of exercises I was to do every day to strengthen my abdominal and gluteal muscles. Once they were strengthened it would take the strain off my back and allow it to heal. I had to swim each day as well, the doctor said, for half an hour. If that didn't work I would have to submit to back surgery in the fall or end up in a wheelchair, or both. I believed him, yet at the same time, I didn't believe him.

SALABHASANA (Locust Pose)

That August I went south to the sea. Each day for a month I did one hundred situps and other exercises to heal my back injury and strengthen my abdominal muscles. I was supposed to swim as often as possible but only the breast stroke, the doctor had cautioned. It would cause the least amount of strain to my injured back. Consumed with anxiety and fearing that I might end up in a wheelchair, I did the back exercises six or seven times a day when I wasn't at the pool breast stroking my way back and forth across the shallow end because I was afraid to swim in water over my head. Harriet O'Toole, the owner of the Seacrest Inn where I was staying, told me months later that they thought the reason I seldom emerged from my room was because I was a serious dope smoker who spent her time doing little else. I decided not to tell them I was exercising and reading cheap novels till five o'clock every morning; they wouldn't have believed it.

On August first, the day I was to leave for the month of exercise and recuperation, I packed lightly since I could barely walk and was too weak to carry anything. My best friend, Jordan, had offered to make the two-hour trip with me for the weekend, to carry my bags onto the train and then from the train to the guest house. On the morning of departure he neither arrived nor answered his phone when I dialed his number. When Carrie called me that morning to say goodbye I told her Jordan hadn't shown up. I heard her cluck in disapproval.

"How are you going to get down there by yourself," she asked.

"I'll manage," I told her.

"I'll come over and take you there myself," she insisted. "Otherwise, how will you get there?"

I hesitated. Hadn't she volunteered to come and scrub out my filthy bathtub when the doctor told me to take hot baths every night to ease the pain of my back injury? Hadn't she actually done it without asking anything of me in return?

The trip was a blur. Once we arrived and she helped me to unpack and put a few of my things away, she began to look smilingly into my eyes and hint broadly about being in love with me. I pretended not to understand her. Her lover, Ruby, telephoned the guest house several times that day, anxious to know what Carrie was doing and asking when she could expect Carrie to arrive home. Jokingly, Carrie put her off, saying that I still needed her help and that she would return on a later train. I preferred to believe that Carrie was helping me out of compassion and feelings of pure friendship. After all, I could barely walk. I was consumed with feelings of anxiety. I had only the month of August in which to rehabilitate myself before back surgery and/or life in a wheelchair. And she wanted me to think about receiving her sexually and maybe loving her too. It was too much to ask.

It would be fifteen years, until the night of the lunar eclipse, before we would act out the scenario that was to be the denouement of this day. I can see, plainly, the moon and the sky through the three bay windows of my fifth-floor apartment.

DHANURASANA (Bow Pose) A stretched bow with a string.

Grasp both ankles with your hands and let your body stretch like a bow ready to be plucked.

MAKARASANA (Crocodile Pose)

It is past midnight. Eyes wide, I am staring openly and fully at the eclipse, which is totally otherworldly and lasts for a long time with its strange green shimmer. The eclipse moves at so infinitesimally slow a pace it appears not to move at all. Although I have read that you are not supposed to look at an eclipse with unprotected eyes, I do it anyway in a kind of willful self-destructiveness.

Carrie and I are stretched on the narrow leather couch in my living room, just opposite the bay windows through which the eclipse hovers; it is a presence in the room. Everyone else in the building has gone to bed, including my lover in her apartment down the hall. Half-clothed, we are twisting and turning and sweating because it is summer, or maybe late spring. Our mouths are glued together in kisses; our hunger is more than sexual. We are both betraying my lover who is her friend: I, because I want revenge for my lover's lack of interest in me; she, because she's wanted to do this for years. Although I know there won't be any sleep for me this night, I continue to stare at the sky as we're undulating together on the couch. I'm perfectly aware that looking into the eclipse is bad karma, but the only thing I seem to care about is to prove to myself that I'm still alive. That nothing else matters, not the green eclipse's unearthly light, not Carrie's thick body, nor Carrie herself whom I neither desire nor regard as anything more than an old friend. The evening began late, with her offer to rub my stiff and sore back for a while. She says she's very good at back rubs, but what I am really engaged in is the spilling and spoilage of my essential energy before the cold radiation of the moon. I do it for warmth, for sex, for life. A little life.

DHANURASANA (Bow Pose) A stretched bow with a string.

Nicole's face was a mask of makeup, her eyebrows torturously plucked. Dressed only in black, she took a book with her whenever she went to bars and sat alone, reading. Reading as if she were simply not interruptible, a drink before her on the table. Her greatest desire was to be thought interesting, to have people in the bar wonder who that solitary woman was, the woman always alone, always reading. What was the book? A French novel? Philosophy? Interesting. When someone asked if they might join her she would decline; it would spoil the image; she had to be alone to create the mystery. Nicole was in love with the Paris of Henry Miller and Anais Nin. In love with both of them as well, but mostly with Nin. That was what we had in common, she thought. Nin.

I had discovered Nin's novels and short stories remaindered at a bookstore in the Village a few years before the publication of Nin's diaries. I'd found her books *Ladders to Fire* and *Spy in the House of Love*, and adored them for their strangeness, the gayness I recognized in them, the stories written to Djuna, her attractions to women, so utterly romanticized they embarrassed even me. Her intensity and passion made me think of my own. It was easy to see how Nicole could get hooked on Nin, even hot for her. Nicole and her husband Tone had driven to New York to Nin's apartment in the Village to meet her. Nicole had even tried to seduce Nin, but Nin had not been interested. "I was broken-hearted, it was too late for me," Nicole whispered that night in my apartment as we sat talking until dawn, her hand on my knee. "It was just too late and I was crushed." I thought Nicole's hand on my knee was a promising sign, to her it seemed to mean nothing.

She'd followed me in a breathless chase in her fancy sportscar, with its leather interior for an hour through the streets of Baltimore, having noticed me in the driver's seat of my car when we were both stopped at a light somewhere downtown late at night. I had just arrived upstairs in my apartment when the doorbell rang. There was Nicole, breathless and big-eyed, smelling strongly of perfume, hovering in my doorway.

"I followed you home because I had to find out where you lived. It was too much of a coincidence that we should pass each other on the street in our cars. I knew I was meant to follow you," she breathed.

Brushing aside my misgivings, I decided to let her in; long earrings, lots of makeup. We sat talking until dawn, her hand on my thigh, now and then, my knee.

I had invited Nin to appear at the College, and she came twice that year, once to read from her stories and another time to show the experimental films of her husband, Ian Hugo. Nicole appeared in my office soon after the first event was announced to explain to me that she knew and adored Nin's work and the Paris of Henry Miller and Nin. She wanted to have a party for Nin after the reading, a party at a friend's house in the suburbs, because, she said, the friend's house was "a beautiful setting" and Nin deserved, no, HAD to be in a beautiful setting. She was that beautiful. Who are these friends? I wanted to know. A beautiful androgynous married couple, Bernie and Stevie, who possessed two "beautiful" childen, and, of course, a "beautiful home."

"Look," I said, "Nin doesn't want to linger after the reading; she wants to leave early to catch her train back to New York. I don't think she'll want to go out to the suburbs. She wants us to provide refreshments at the College after the reading so she can leave from there." Exasperated, Nicole could see I didn't grasp the importance of her aesthetics of the event. Didn't understand.

"Don't you see she's too beautiful for this ugly school setting. I want her to experience the beauty of the home of my friends, the perfect setting for her. I'll drive her there in my sportscar and drive her to the station afterwards."

She asked me for Nin's phone number so she could call and ask her directly, but I was under strict orders to give it to no one. When Nin replied in the negative, Nicole was furious. After the reading she went into a corner with Nin for as long as Nin would allow, and that was when she must have arranged to visit Nin in New York.

After that she came to my office to visit, to chat, and we began to go out occasionally. I was lonely; she had appeared. But those eager looks, that passionate breathlessness of the first night's visit quickly disappeared.

ARDHA-HALASANA (Half-Plow Pose)

When I dialed the number, the phone rang four times. Then there was a pause. I could hear a woman's voice hum a little, as if testing her voice for the tape. Then she cleared her throat—hem hem. Then she began her taped message, "I want a woman. I want a woman in the White House. I want a woman in The Senate. I want a woman in The House of Representatives. I want a woman to make laws, to make policies, to . . ." There was a good deal more, but it all went by me except for the "I want a woman" part. The long speech—long for a tape message—ended with the words, "I want a woman." The message played whenever I dialed the number, which on some days was often. There was frequently nobody home at the house of Colleen's sister or else they screened every call. Sasha was having an affair with Colleen with whom she'd had a three-month affair twelve years earlier. Colleen, who lived in L.A., made regular visits to Baltimore, this visit allegedly to attend her son's college graduation. Colleen had been trying unsuccessfully for years to get Sasha hooked on her again and this time she had picked the right moment. An old friend of Sasha's had just died of cancer. At the moment of

Colleen's arrival, Sasha's mind was on the fleetingness of life and the importance of grasping whatever pleasures presented themselves before they got away or you passed on. She let herself be easily seduced by Colleen's late-night phone calls, her flowers, her sending of tapes of Judy Collins crooning "It's not over till it's over," her volley of love letters most of which I found and read and wept over, since Sasha made no great effort to hide them. When she was confronted with them, Sasha laughed and said they didn't mean a thing, not to worry. And besides, she would always add, this time it was for certain, over. Colleen was staying at her sister's house in Wilmington. Whenever I didn't know where Sasha was, which was often, I'd dial the number, desperate to find her. Each time I dialed, I'd hear the taped voice of Colleen's sister, a woman I didn't know, clear her throat and test out her voice by humming first, then bursting into the message, "I want a woman." I'd cringe at the sound. But Sasha probably didn't cringe, she probably liked it. Maybe she was just in the mood to like it. I couldn't banish the thought that Sasha liked this crassness and everything else about Colleen that was unlike me, including Colleen's "I want a woman" sister with her Sunday-afternoon chicken barbecue.

"Would you like to meet Colleen?" Sasha asked eagerly. "Tonight? She's at the bar. You could meet her; she could meet you." Sasha's eyes glittered, her breath came short and fast. I could see the excitement on her face at the sound of Colleen's name in her mouth. She seemed intoxicated.

"No," was what I said. "No." I felt sick. My own style was not right in Sasha's eyes now and perhaps would never be again. That phone message was really her speed.

I could tell Sasha had been thrashing about in her soul for weeks over her recently deceased friend. She was in the process of selling her business to one of her associates, something she had been planning in detail for a long time. In the eleven years in which I'd known Sasha there was never a time when she didn't have a goal, whereas I just lived.

One day as I took a seat on the bus and crossed one leg over the other, the realization came over me:

She doesn't want you.

I had had the identical thought about Sasha before, but I'd always dismissed it. Suddenly it was true. Hadn't I literally begged Sasha for sex on my previous birthday? Hadn't she ignored me? With trepidation, I decided to ask her again. Of course it wasn't forthcoming; of course I knew it wouldn't be. What she said with a little smile was, "Shall we have a little lickey-lick then?" I was repelled by her false playfulness and her tone. As the day drew to a close, she made no movement towards me. I made no movement towards her. Sasha had lost her desire for me; I felt it. If I was ever again to be physically, sexually loved, it would have to be with someone other than Sasha.

Who would want this damaged body, I thought. *A woman past her prime. This body—sere, dry, wounded from not being loved.*

Who?

There was no answer and I expected none.

The idea of my body, which could so easily feel erotic, even electric with desire, being separated forever from those feelings was too much to bear. Too much to accept. A body full of life and the ability to tremble with desire to be cut off, not from desire, but from the warm and silky welcoming hands and body of response; a lover.

The fact that I was no longer attractive to Sasha—even though I knew Sasha didn't have what it took to make me come—did not stop me from loving and desiring her. I had faked orgasms in the eleven years we had been together because I knew Sasha's pride could not accept failure. I was good at faking. Sasha lacked my patience, which often seemed to me to be endless. Her arm or her hand would grow tired. She would give up, say she had a cramp in her neck or back; I never felt Sasha would see me through. In fact I knew she would not, though, of course, Sasha expected me to see her through, to be there for her. I loved Sasha enough, I enjoyed the power of making her come in my arms, no matter how long or what it took.

Eleven years, I thought.

Eleven.

I knew I could not give Sasha up, I was dependent on her, addicted to her. But I was starved for the power that sex, the aliveness, the wholeness—gave me. I began consciously to yearn for someone—a lover—who could give me what Sasha would not.

I began to dwell on it.

I remembered the story an old friend, a social worker, had told me about one of her clients, a woman who made love to women for money. I'm really good at it, the woman confessed in her therapy session. Really good, you know, talented, I make good money. But don't you think it would be better for me to look for some other kind of work? Do you think this is good for me? she asked my friend.

God, I thought, if only I could find her! I fantasized about being held, stroked, and carefully made love to by a lover whose pleasure it was to slowly but surely draw my senses together in a delicious way that would make me come. I couldn't imagine what this unknown, unknowable woman would be like and whether or not I'd like sex as business. For money. I rather thought I wouldn't be able to relax in it.

The idea of a stranger whose husky whisper would give me orders, utter the words, "No matter what, I'm not letting you slip out of my hands." She would lavish on me the sensation I wanted. This body needs watering, needs to be loved, I said to myself.

I began to dwell on the idea of a woman other than Sasha whose arms and mouth and hands would give me the sensations I craved.

I put my desire into the universe.

I opened myself.

I waited.

Journal of the Year of the Woodboar

January 12, 1995

Every large and small thing there was to learn in the world, the lessons of pleasure and pain, she has learned on her body.

Two years of studying Classical Chinese Herbology have taught her that Chinese herbs can treat her major problems: insomnia and a lump she has found in her breast. She thinks that if anything works it will be this system of logic and mystery that ineluctably draws her because its purpose is to go to the root of things. Which is also hers. Chinese Medicine.

She has gone to the Chinese doctor for treatment.

Within a few seconds Doris knows in her gut that Hongwei Zhu, the Chinese doctor who wants her patients to just call her "Hongwei," is a goddess of needles and herbs, a bear-woman. Her mind takes more time to know.

It is not long before early spring and the Chinese New Year.

Doris feels a stirring within her body, maybe from the raw Chinese herbs she has gotten from Hongwei who tells her, "boil herbs together, simmer for one hour, drain out liquid and save; boil and simmer again, drain, mix liquids; drink one cup morning, one cup night each bag two days. Heat up first."

According to the Chinese Law of The Five Elements, the kidneys, which control all of the water in the body, also control the fire of the heart.

Yong-Li, her teacher of Chinese medicine, has told her that her insomnia is caused by the overpowering of her kidneys by her heart fire, a major imbalance. Dr. Louie Chang, an acupuncturist and herbalist whose advertisement she sees and answers in the *Village Voice* has said that excessive heart fire is overpowering her kidneys. Now, when Hongwei explains the problem to her in more vague but similar terms, Doris thinks nothing could be a more powerful symbol for her than that the Houses of Fire and Water—as these are called—are doing battle inside her.

Yong-Li has explained that the kidneys, which are the seat of the will, control all things which can easily go out of control. If heart fire, for instance, is overpowering the kidney waters, you cannot sleep; the fire will keep you awake. That is what taking the Chinese herbs will finally get to the root of—the imbalance between her houses of fire and water.

The heart houses the soul, the spirit, which is known in Chinese medicine as the Shen. When the shen is broken, the rest of the emotions are out of control forever, because, Yong-Li explains, the function of the shen is to keep all of the emotions in place. Doris can't recall when she felt the original breaking of her shen; there were many after the first.

Mending the shen is a different matter. Yong-Li has said in class, in answer to her question—of course she would be the one to have asked the question—that, yes, it is possible but difficult to heal a broken shen.

For the possibility of mending the shen, Doris wants to include Hongwei in her cohort of Mistresses of the Animals—the mothers of her soul.

Both her deepest and her most upwards memories of the earth and her history are needed so she can feel herself shoot far down into The Underworld, then be able to rise from the chaos, healed. More than anyone, Doris most wants Hongwei to understand that their spiritual lives are linked, but she knows she can't explain it; it is not something Hongwei wants to know. Doris envisions the roots of plants that will begin to stir in the deep cold of February. She knows she herself is meant to water people's roots. In ways they don't expect or ask for. But want.

She dreams this choreography: that she enters a scene carrying a large glass pitcher. She waters people's roots. Her own roots are being turned up, laid down, and watered at the same time.

The putting together with water and fire, the element of the heart—the shen, the soul—this is all a part of Hongwei with her needles and herbs, and her knowledge of healing. But she can't just say, Hongwei, 1201, the number on your office door is the same as the number of the apartment I lived in for thirteen years; we are somehow connected in this healing process, maybe you are the key. She can't figure out a way to explain it in an appropriate fashion and maybe Hongwei will just get it if her mind would only work that way but Doris doubts that it does.

January 16

In spare moments on the train to New York, Doris reads and rereads her Chinese Medicine notes:

Insomnia:

> The amount and quality of sleep depend on the state of mind or shen. The shen is rooted in the heart, specifically in the heart blood and heart yin. If the heart is healthy and blood abundant, the shen will be rooted and sleep will be sound. If the heart is deficient or if it is agitated by pathogenic factors such as fire, the shen will not be properly rooted and sleep will be affected. The length and quality of sleep are also related to the state of the ethereal soul, the hun, different from the shen, and rooted in the liver. If liver blood or liver yin is deficient, the ethereal soul or hun will not be anchored and will wander, causing restless sleep and tiring dreams.
>
> Worrying and excessive thinking injure the spleen so that it cannot make blood and insomnia results. Heart blood is directly weakened by worry. In some people, worry, anxiety and pensiveness lead to heart fire which flares upward to agitate the mind and insomnia results. Heart fire flaring up and failing to communicate downwards with the kidneys leads to kidney yin deficiency, as excessive heart fire injures the yin. Long-term kidney yin deficiency fails to nourish heart yin, so that heart empty heat develops. This is called disharmony between the heart and the kidneys.

January 18, 1995

Looking down at the chart in her hands, Hongwei says, "It is very nice to see you, Doris." Her voice is warm, deep and resonant. Singsong. "It is very nice to see you."

Thick black lashes and eyebrows. Extreme shyness. Doris feels oddly, absurdly and very clearly as if she is in love. But this cannot be.

January 24, 1995

It is nineteen degrees fahrenheit outside.

Without uttering a word, Hongwei enters the examining room, reaches over and takes Doris's hand, to check the level of its warmth or coldness. This is a quick way to tell if her kidney yang or spleen yang is deficient because the extremities always show the internal condition.

Without thinking, Doris closes her hand lightly back around Hongwei's. Hongwei instantly yanks her hand from Doris's and takes two steps backwards.

Overstepped boundaries, Doris thinks. She knows she took the hand as it was proffered. She feels shame at Hongwei's reaction.

Hongwei is more formal than usual today. The son of a Chinese colleague is visiting to observe her, a short, fat man who is already balding although he can't be more than thirty-five. Observing him, Doris thinks automatically, on the basis of Oriental diagnosis, *excess yin intake.*

Hongwei takes her pulses and tells Doris, "You are much better than last week. Less stressed out. More calm today." She smiles. Her short thick hair is worn Chinese style over her ears which are completely hidden. Against the cold, Hongwei wears a pale green mock turtle sweater of wool and an ankle-length black skirt.

Something about Hongwei's energy and the tone of her voice charges Doris's emotions. Speeds her pulse. She sees through Hongwei's polite manner fire, intense, internal, like her own. Heart fire. It comes across as formalness, though it is not meant to be. Doris finds herself slowing her speech. She feels Hongwei grappling with the language and her own leading of Hongwei to what she is trying to say. Hongwei's speech stumbles a good deal. Often she says "he" when she means "she" and doesn't notice the difference. But sometimes, her speech is smooth and fluent, a function of stress, probably, or greater familiarity with the set of phrases she is using.

Doris stands before the triple windows in Hongwei's office that look out over the crisscrossing downtown streets. She observes the church spires and carved gargoyles which she might possibly be able to touch if she could just reach out her hand to them.

Hongwei begins to fill her prescription by opening jars and taking out the correct number of grams of herbs. Her palm knows perfectly the weights of each of the herbs as she pours from her fingers fourteen different herbal substances onto the tops of six magazine covers laid out for that purpose. Six magazine covers; six bags. One week's worth for Doris to take. Skip one day. When she is finished, Hongwei lifts up and partially rolls shut each magazine cover, points its end into a small paper bag, slides in the contents and staples shut the top of the bag. Banging the jar hard against the floor—one-two-three—is the way she loosens any hard-to-open jar-lids. She grabs a hammer and smashes off big chunks of the herbs that are dried hard and stiff, against the floor, having first kicked closed her desk drawer to make space for this banging and smashing.

Big fire nature, Doris thinks.

Hongwei wears a small gold heart around her neck on a gold chain, and a small pretty bracelet on her left wrist. As Hongwei lightly presses the three pulses on each of Doris's wrists, slowly, carefully, Doris is aware of the heat of Hongwei's hands and the pressure of each finger on her wrists; one side, then the other. She looks at this face with what Hongwei must register as a searching glance that travels caressingly, but not, she hopes, intrusively around her eyes, face and mouth.

"Digestion not so good?" Her fingers on Doris's right wrist.

"I guess so."

"Sleep isn't so good either? Energy not so good either," she finishes.

"I have pretty low energy."

"From your flu virus?"

"Yes," Doris replies. "Can you give me acupuncture to open up the pressure in my ears?"

"The best way to relieve the pressure in your ears is with herbs. Although I've prepared your herbs for your breast nodule, I haven't prepared them for your virus because that's new information."

"These herbs won't just take away my symptoms, will they?" Doris says, "because that will drive the virus deeper inside my body."

"No, they will help you."

Doris wants to ask exactly what the herbs will do then, but says instead, "O.K., I trust you." She doesn't know why she says this; trust is not one of the feelings she has for Hongwei.

"Take your herbs one half-hour before eating, not with food and not right after eating. You are retaining water," Hongwei says. "Are your fingers or ankles swollen?"

Doris emphasizes that they are not and holds up her legs a few inches from the floor so that Hongwei can see her ankles. Hongwei repeats, "According to your pulses, you are retaining water."

Doris wants to check her own knowledge. "Hongwei, if my pulses are slippery, isn't that a definite sign of damp heat? Wouldn't that mean that my major condition right now is damp heat? I look up the herbs you give me in the Chinese Materia Medica each week so I can tell from their properties what conditions you are prescribing for."

She is never certain Hongwei understands what she is saying, but she continues to speak, slowing herself down when she sees Hongwei's eyes begin to dart to catch her meaning. At the end of this speech Hongwei responds.

"Damp heat." She nods, "Yes. No. Yes."

"Which is it Hongwei, yes or no?"

Hongwei looks at her uncertainly. "What you call it? In English?"

"Damp heat."

"Sure. Damp heat. That's right."

January 30, 1995

On the day of her first visit to Hongwei, with Doris lying half-naked, her upper body covered with a cold sheet on Hongwei's examining table, Hongwei suddenly commences pacing back and forth, the smile gone from her face. She has just finished lecturing Doris on the way great stress for too long a time makes liver blood stagnation—a condition which has helped create the breast mass she now has—and breast masses for women in general. Doris cannot recall a time when she has not felt great stress in many years. She lies listening to Hongwei's voice and what she is saying when, as if in a trance, Hongwei begins, with no introduction, to describe how, in her eleventh year, the Chinese Communists tore her from her home in Shanghai and sent her and other children by truck to the countryside, and made them work in the fields with no food, no shelter, no clothing except what they were wearing on their backs. After they worked in the fields for days, they were given not quite enough rice to sustain them and had to perform backbreaking labor for many hours to receive even small amounts of food.

"I want die. I want kill myself," intones Hongwei. "We have no food. Nothing to eat. We're starving. I want die. I just want die." Her eyes are clouded and dark, her brows knit. "There is no food for anyone, not even cats or dogs. You have to go to bathroom in fields, just out in open. Dogs, cats come to eat what you make as it comes from your body. There is no place to go. Everyone starving. I want die. I want kill myself."

Doris feels struck. Why has Hongwei chosen to tell her, a complete stranger, this personal tale on her first office visit? She wonders if Hongwei tells the story to all of her new patients, or if she has been specially chosen. To her, the story is about shame, about the breaking of Hongwei's shen in her eleventh year. She thinks Hongwei wants her to take part in the healing of her shen, just as Doris has chosen Hongwei to help heal her own. Her mind is fascinated with such equations. *Too fascinated,* she thinks.

Hongwei's voice softens and becomes less serious as she draws closer to her usual persona but is not quite there. "I don't die. I come home. My parents come back Shanghai. After a while everything turn out O.K.

She seems to return to herself. "I go to make your herbs," she says. You get dressed. Take time."

February 4
A telephone conversation between Hongwei and Doris
"You have such a beautiful life, Doris; you're so busy. That's good. Very good."

(What is meant here by 'beautiful'? Doris wonders.)

"I have no time for anything in my life except to work. I don't get home until nine-thirty or ten o'clock every night. I can rest only one day a week."

Doris's voice interrupts Hongwei's litany of too much work, work all the time, no rest.

"Hongwei, you are very successful; maybe you shouldn't worry so much about getting patients. About business." Doris doesn't use the word worried, she says "work so hard. Your patients love you, Hongwei, you are a great success!"

Hongwei makes a choked-up sound like "no no no," but Doris plunges on.

"You are a success, Hongwei, you should be able to relax a little now. Not worry about your office all the time."

But Hongwei continues talking about how hard she works, how hard her life is.

"On which day do you rest, Hongwei?"

"Sunday is the only day that I have to rest."

"You have great drive, Hongwei," Doris concludes, "because you are a very yang person."

"No. I am not," Hongwei declares. "I am not yang."

"What I mean is, your profession is yang."

There is a slight pause. "No. It is not." A very firm voice.

No, it is not yang, not aggressive to push needles into people's skin; nor is it exact, contracted, highly focused. Hongwei's well-modulated voice is also loud. *None of these things.*

"Okay," Doris says. "Not yang. You are not yang."

"When you go to New York, do you go by train, or do you drive?" Hongwei has asked her this more than once.

"I take the train."

Because Doris has told her she goes to New York every week to study Classical Chinese Herbology, nearly every time Hongwei sees or talks to Doris she wants to know, "Going to New York?" or "Did you just come from New York?"

"Tomorrow," Doris will answer. Or "Yesterday."

Today Doris has wonderful news.

"This weekend I am going to New York to see the New York City Ballet. Dance is one of my great passions!" She's bursting with energy. She tosses in the last sentence to try to convey to Hongwei her love for dance, her excitement about it, her joy.

"I'm going to stay in a hotel so I can go to the theatre two nights in a row."

On the other end of the telephone Hongwei sighs. "You have such a beautiful life; what a beautiful life you have Doris! I, I work all the time. Study. Am always in the office, working. I can never go to New York or anywhere. Even at home on Sunday I am busy making formulas for my patients. I am working, always working."

Again, Doris cannot tell what 'beautiful life' means to Hongwei, but she thinks it is shorthand for something that does not mean 'beautiful' in the Western sense. She is waiting for Hongwei to explain to her the meaning of the state she calls 'beautiful life.' Their conversation feels to Doris like it's hurtling down an unknown road.

Hongwei hastens on with her tale. "I didn't even have time to be pregnant. Only two months to spend with my daughter fourteen years ago. I was in school. I had to work, study all the time."

Doris wants to ask if she was married when she was pregnant, but asks instead if she had anyone to help her with the baby when she was in medical school. "Did your mother help with the baby Hongwei?"

"Yes, my mother helped me out."

"Your daughter, is she with you now or is she in China?"

"She is here with me."

Doris notices that Hongwei makes no mention of a husband.

February 8, 1995

Hongwei's formal greeting is: "My very good friend." She addresses Doris without looking at her.

"Why don't you study here instead of going to New York?"

"There is no school here."

"Why don't you open a school?"

"What?"

"So I can teach here."

Her hands on Doris's wrists are hot and warm at the same time. She hoists herself up on the edge of the examining table, her seated body nudged against Doris's prone torso. Doris is listening to her but not hearing her.

Dressed in starched white pants and pointy, low-heeled, black shoes, Hongwei drops her eyes when Doris stares at her. Doris, further enticed by this refusal, stares at this Chinese face that she finds beautiful. Stares at the planes of Hongwei's face, her flat nose, her eyes, her eyebrows, the hands with finely tapered fingers which, each and every week that Doris lies in a prone position on this table, feel both of Doris's breasts, first to compare them and then to see if the lump Doris has in her left breast has diminished by virtue of her taking the herbal formula. Stares at her face, no holds barred, fascinated by her otherness, her sameness.

Hongwei likes to be stared at.

ALS—Lou Gehrig's disease—is one of Hongwei's clinical specialties. After she gave a talk at Mears Hospital on the subject to a group of people who suffer from the disease, Hongwei's assistant, Jeanette, tells Doris most of the group became her patients. A large number then? Doris wants to know, curious about anything that has to do with Hongwei. No, a total of only four or five, all of whom seem to benefit from taking Hongwei's herbs.

On some days Hongwei seems thin and wiry. One day when she wears a short skirt underneath her white coat Doris notices that her calves are very well-developed. From standing on her feet so much, Doris thinks, or riding a bicycle as a student in Shanghai.

Soon after that Doris notices that Hongwei begins to wear ankle-length skirts.

February 14, 1995

"You are very stressed today—much more than last week. As much as the first day you came to see me!" Hongwei scolds in a loud voice. Doris accepts this motherly tone and hopes that Hongwei can't read too much into her heart pulse. That she is, of course, part of the stress Doris feels, the best part. *You have no secrets from Chinese doctors*, Doris thinks. *They read your pulses, your tongue, your face, your skin, read you all the way through. Oriental diagnosis makes you too much like an open book.* She dislikes the feeling of not being able to choose her secrets. But maybe only a few of the best Oriental medicine doctors can read you that well. She doesn't know if Hongwei is actually one of the best.

"Your nodule is softer. Do you feel a pressure?"

"You mean a pressure in the breast from the nodule?"

"Yes."

"No."

"Feel any pain?"

"No."

Pale-green blouse. White starched pants. White lab coat. Pointy, low-heeled, black shoes.

The first time Hongwei directs her to go in and remove

everything to the waist and lie down on her back on the examining table, Doris does not know what to expect. At the moment that Hongwei comes in, she quickly covers Doris's chest with the folded sheet; as she lifts it and places her hands on Doris's breasts, Doris closes her eyes. She wants the feeling of Hongwei's hands on her breasts but forces herself to immediately open her eyes. To not allow Hongwei, who is intently watching her face, see how much she wants this. To not allow herself to be in so vulnerable a position.

Yet for a moment she wants to be just what she is feeling, not care whether or not it is appropriate. Just be it. But she stares at a space just below the ceiling, a serious expression on her face. Hongwei's face has the same expression while her hands linger very professionally on the left breast. "Pretty much same size as last time. No change."

She tells Doris she will be right back, for Doris to get dressed.

February 18, 1995
Journal entry
Lying in bed under the ceiling my brain ablaze with light I feel my body expand in flame, see my head and my hands sprouting green, a conduit, the seeds planted in me by magic, without my knowledge or asking. Nothing still when you see me. Flickering.

February 28
Doris feels expertly nailed with a ring of needles on her upper back (bladder meridian) and three more in her left and right ear, the Shenmen, heart and liver points. "For your emotional problems," is Hongwei's laconic explanation, wording straight from the acupuncture textbook. Doris feels bared by the statement. An accusation.

I don't have emotional problems, she wants to reply, but she knows there are few secrets Chinese medicine can't fathom, though the interpretation of them can often be wrong.

Coming out of the examining room, she leans against the doorjamb of Hongwei's office like she's melting from the effects of the acupuncture treatment. Like she can't stand straight. A sleepy, slowed-down feeling that doesn't last long enough for her. Seated at her desk, Hongwei sees Doris in the doorway and says "Come in. Sit down," or "have seat." She doesn't look directly at Doris at first.

Then, becoming all warmth and charm she exclaims suddenly, "I want you try out my new teas. They are all same herbs, just ground down into powder and put in teabags. Much easier to take. Just boil and simmer for ten minutes, then drink."

Doris can see the rows of big glass jars with raw herbs in them on the shelves of Hongwei's open closet.

"I prefer the traditional way," Doris says. "The raw herbs are stronger and more appropriate for breast lumps, aren't they Hongwei? My herbology teachers say this." She wants the purest, strongest remedies, not some watered-down Americanized version of Chinese Medicine.

"O.K., I respect your wish," Hongwei says. "You want traditional way. It is best. But my patients tell me ground herbs are easier because there is no need to cook. I know my American patients. They want that. They don't have time to cook. Too busy. But you want traditional way. O.K. I respect your wish."

Doris wonders if Hongwei has really heard her.

Before she departs, Hongwei takes her aside and admonishes, "Since you are improving it would be okay for you to take the ground-up herbs now even though they are less strong."

Doris shakes her head. She wants the raw herbs only. Fifteen minutes earlier they had agreed on this.

Hongwei makes her voice soothing and sensuous. She smiles and nods at Doris. "I respect your wish, Doris; I respect your wish. Because you respect nature. I understand. I give you what you want."

Six small teabags in a bag with Doris's name on it await her at her next visit. Hongwei tells her, "Just try, see if you like. If don't like, you can go back to raw herbs after two weeks."

Doris takes them. She is annoyed, but she laughs at the same time.

March 3, 1995

She has the authority in her hands Doris wants in a lover.

Hongwei decides today that Doris should have acupuncture to help "unblock the meridian channels." In spite of Doris's knowledge that Chinese herbal prescriptions are the best treatment for breast masses, she agrees to let Hongwei do the needling.

Doris has always acted out on the bodies of her lovers what she wanted from them. Mostly they refused to understand, doing instead whatever they pleased. Which was seldom what she wanted and had, she thought, made perfectly clear. Her anger at this, which built into suppressed rage over a long period of time, created massive liver qi and liver blood stagnation—the root cause of breast lumps, according to Chinese Medicine, as Hongwei has told her more than once.

"You were sooo—ah—agitate, ah—agitated for such a long time. You need relax. It will take long time, these herbs. Because for so many years you suffer such stress in your life. For many women that is the cause of their—ah—breast lumps and nodules. Too much stress and worrying. Suppressed anger. You have had this for many, many years. And, from your profession; you stay up late at night doing work with your ah—mind. That causes your problem, too. Not good for you do mental work after midnight. You don't need change your profession. Just change habits."

Doris feels Hongwei direct the needles into the skin of her back, the little thump as each needle emerges from its individual holder

She is in a Chinese doctor's office, half nude, being punctured with needles, an ancient technique that is supposed to cure. She has given herself up to the authority of Hongwei's aim. For the moment. She knows she is allowing, no, wanting herself to feel more than the just the needles puncturing her skin, the heat lamp being placed nearby to warm her, the soft Oriental music being turned on to soothe her mind for the half hour she will lie there with needles in her back. She has discovered that being near Hongwei, talking with her—anything—for any amount of, makes her wet and she is amazed at this. She thinks it might be connected with the macrobiotic dietary adjustments she has made, or with the Chinese herbs she drinks each day or the occasional acupuncture, but that it is more likely a combustion that takes place within her body and mind.

She doesn't really know.

She has uncomfortably, unhappily accepted the possibility that this essential condition of wetness, the ability to receive and give love has gone from her.

She asks no one about it, mentions it to no one, thinks it is her fate—the result of the long-term emotional excesses of her nature. Yet now she feels unmistakably alive and moist, and there is nothing else on earth that produces this but her proximity to Hongwei. She is amazed and grateful. There is no one to whom she can tell this story, least of all, Hongwei.

Hongwei has been raised to be hardworking, a proper Chinese professional woman. To seem reliable. To deal with life business first, heart never. Knows how to handle herself. Can be relied on to be acceptable and mainstream, even if not straightforward, if not a minor stretching of the truth, a bit of wheeling and dealing or outright lying when the need arises.

Doris has been raised to deal—heart, period. Not business. Raised to not know what is expected of her by parents absorbed in grief, a brother absorbed in his sexuality, a sister absorbed in madness. Raised to deal with the covertness, the secrets of other people as facts she is outside of, can never know except maybe in her gut. Which feels like it is wrong at least fifty percent of the time, although she can make herself half crazy thinking how can a feeling be wrong; it can't.

She has been raised wild.

March 9, 1995

She can't stand up straight; she is in pain from having twisted her back. She calls Hongwei's office to ask for acupuncture treatment for the pain. Jeanette tells her to come in at 12:30, her voice full of concern. Doris hears somehow in Jeanette's tone that she is considered special, a special patient by Hongwei, and thus by Jeanette. But then maybe she speaks this way to each person, so that everyone is given the illusion they are special.

It is a relief to relax into feeling just pain instead of the usual complicated feelings she has for Hongwei. While she is preparing to leave, she asks how long it will take before the acupuncture will take effect. Hongwei says the pain will melt away in three days, that it will just melt away. Jeanette later confides to her that the words "melt away" are the most poetic she has ever heard from Hongwei.

Doris stands facing Hongwei in the doorway of her office as she is about to leave. "How tall are you Hongwei? Sometimes you seem much taller than I am and sometimes you seem exactly my height."

"On some days I'm bigger, on some days I'm smaller. I don't know why." Hongwei shrugs.

"For me too. On some days . . ." Doris inhales, fills her lungs, her arms falsely big, encircling a large round ball of air like she's embracing the world. Watching her closely, Hongwei nods her head rapidly. "And sometimes . . . ." here Doris crunches her chest and arms inwards to make the gesture of smallness. Hongwei nods again.

Bigger or smaller, whatever the day provides.

"Are you five three?" Doris asks. Hongwei repeats the words "five three" after Doris, then says, "five four." Like she doesn't know which.

"All I do is work," she says suddenly. "My life is too much work. I work six days. The only day I have off is Sunday. I have nothing else in my life but work. When I am home I have to grind the herbs to bring to the office for my patients.

"When I go home at night I am so hungry I don't care what is there; I just grab it out of the refrigerator and eat. I even eat meat!" she bursts out looking guardedly at Doris.

"But you," she adds, "you don't do that." She hesitates and looks at Doris with an expression Doris can't read. Something about wanting approval and fearing that Doris will not give it.

"You are so well-organized, you would never do that."

"Of course I do it sometimes." Doris says. She observes that Hongwei wants to view her as a model of proper eating behavior. She is surprised at this.

Eye-to-eye, they share the feeling of hunger and the need to assuage it.

"There is too much of me. I am too heavy." She points vaguely to her mid-section, which is covered by her white lab coat.

Doris tells her there is a certain diet she can follow where she can eat all she wants and never gain a pound. It is called Macrobiotics.

"Really!" Hongwei flashes a big smile. "Give it to me on a piece of paper so I can read it."

Goddess of needles and roots, she writes on the back of an envelope she will soon misplace. *Goddess of seeds, of barks that reach into the liver, cool down the heart. Goddess of. Goddess of . . .*

She doesn't know.

On the train to New York, she is surrounded with papers, her fists full of what she regards as the map of her body, her notes on Chinese Medicine. The map is jammed full, the meanings wrung out of the words. She can't let go of it. She is not empty.

An ancient ritual prayer forms in her mouth:

Hongwei, here to fertilize my soil, make me wet
Make me wet, Hongwei, fertilize my soil.

March 15, 1995

Fixing her gaze fully on Doris and speaking in the gentlest of tones, Hongwei asks her how long she has been waiting. Gone is the hesitation, the searching for the right word. The he/she stutter gone. In its place a deep gaze into Doris's face, trying to read every detail of her emotions. Doris isn't unhappy; she is dizzy, she is grateful. If the assistants have kept her waiting without notifying Hongwei of Doris's arrival, so much the better. Doris can spend a few more moments in Hongwei's presence.

Imaginary address to Hongwei

I see you as a strong and beautiful woman whom I have known before. Known you somewhere else and known you well. We have shared the number 1201. You are as familiar to me as myself, yet you are full of unknowns, the erotic and the tranquil. But you are not tranquil. Never tranquil.

I am your mirror, Hongwei. I am your mirror.

Doris addresses Hongwei: "In my last week's herbs, there was no red peony flower."

Hongwei looks startled, as if she is about to jump up from the seat. As if she doesn't know what Doris is saying. But Doris quickly adds, hesitating for only a moment to give it its correct Chinese pronunciation: *"sher shao?"*

"Oh," Hongwei replies immediately, *"shershao!* I don't understand. It was missing from your prescription?" Doris feels Hongwei's fire energy shoot out at her.

Fast, rapid, "The extra bag of herbs I picked up Monday had sher shao in it. But remember last Friday I called to say that I had burnt a pot of my herbs and had to come in Monday morning to pick up another bag? The six bags I got last week had no shershao, it was missing. There was a mistake."

"I made that one for you Monday after you called."

"I know you did. That one was right."

"But the other ones—that was my fault, my fault," Hongwei says immediately.

Because Doris has been kept waiting a few minutes, and one of her main herbs was missing from last week's herb bags, Hongwei, her beautiful face glowing, offers Doris the best of her gifts.

"I will give you acupuncture for your low-back pain with no extra charge."

"It's all right," Doris says. "I came a little late; I didn't have to wait that long." Her lower back doesn't bother her at the moment; she is not fond of needles. "It isn't necessary."

"It is my gift to you. I want give you acupuncture."

The thought of Hongwei inserting needles into her back; the thought of her bare skin under Hongwei's—no—not hands, *needles* at the moment of so much feeling for Hongwei is too much for Doris.

"I accept," she says.

"From now on," Hongwei adds, her face turns earnest," I will personally prepare your herbs each time because you are my long-term patient."

The next time, Hongwei's assistant prepares the herbs for Doris as usual.

March 18, 1995

One afternoon in New York, before going to her Chinese Herbology class, Doris has dinner with her classmate Marina, a student of Chinese medicine and part-time astrologer. Doris asks her to read her astrological chart, which has been mapped out for her by another astrologer. There isn't much time. Marina gives her some quick impressions.

Marina's quick impressions on Doris's natal astrological chart.

Your energies are scattered around the zodiac. A typical jack-of-all-trades chart, not necessarily master of none. Many interests above and below the horizon.

<u>1st House:</u> *Your personality, your physical self. Ruled by the moon, the fastest moving of the planets. Constant changes for you. Can make you moody, changeable.*

<u>2nd House:</u> *Ruled by the sun and Mars, the spendthrift of the zodiac; with it conjunct Neptune, you could be spacy about your money. The sun in the house signifies you are the boss in your work.*

<u>3rd House:</u> *Neptune. House of communication. Neptune, a dreamy mind, not all there. Hated regular school. Dreamed your way through, maybe writing poetry. Films. Drugs. Jupiter and Neptune in the same house. Jupiter rules abundance, so a lot of writing, trips.*

4th House: *Venus rules this, your home house. Good house karma. You wait on people, make them feel comfortable. Venus is kindness, goodness, love. Flowers in the home. Venus in Scorpio; intense, emotional nature about love. Scorpio is Pluto's sign. Pluto the digger, wants to get to the root of things, does what it has to do, period. Doesn't give up.*

5th House: *Rules sex, love affairs, children, your social life, having a good time. The sun is here so these things important to you. This house, ruled also by Mars and Pluto, intensifies your sexual nature. Loved ones very important to you but you don't want them to order you around.*

6th House: *Work, your interest in health/sickness. Jupiter rules here. Outgoing. Like Santa Claus. Ruled by Sagittarius is always happy. You have a saving grace with regard to health problems. Jupiter rules abundance; you have abundant interest in matters governed by this house, thus macrobiotics, Chinese medicine, etc. These interests make you happy, are good for you but—a tendency to do too much.*

7th House: *Marriage, partnerships, competitors, clients. Saturn and the moon rule here and are both in Aquarius, the oddball of the zodiac. Insight into trends before others. Might be done with it before the rest of the world catches on . . . Might be perceived as weird, but get vindicated with time. Saturn/moon gives you depression but it comes and goes. You would want marriage, but also fear it. Where there is Saturn there is fear. Partner gives you security, very important to you, but there is coldness between you at times. If you have clients, they will get their money's worth from you.*

8th House: *Another house of money. Legacies, social security, taxes and death. Unexpected gifts of money.*

9th House: *Ruled by Pisces and Neptune (dreamy, idealistic) which is ruled by Jupiter (happy and benevolent). Travel, publishing, advertising, teaching. Being before the public.*

10th House: *Your mother, career and reputation ruled by the same house, Uranus, makes for a strange mother. Mars also rules, so you have a lot of energy. Not a particularly happy time with your mother. Unexpected things going on with career; sudden happenings. Maybe perceived as being "out there" when it comes to your career, but you are just ahead of your time.*

11th House: *Venus rules this your house of friends. You have loving friends, friends that probably bring you flowers.*

12th House: *This house rules institutions, disappointments, secrets, things behind closed doors. Ruled by Pluto, the intense digger into things, this is the house you want when you write; it gives you the ability to shut everything out. The house you would use to keep your own or someone else's secrets.*

Need progressed chart to show changes from natal chart. Trouble with scattered energies all your life. Right here in your chart.

March 19, 1995

Doris notices today that Hongwei's eyebrows, which she first saw as a thick swatch, a blur over the eye, are in reality a fine line and shaped like her eyes, and that her lips are a deep red, with perhaps a touch of lipstick, her mouth well-shaped and cut full.

March 20, 1995

Notes from a Dakini card divination reading—a Tibetan method.
ARIES. Points the way with a knife and throws it. That is Aries energy; finding the will within to create something entirely new out of yourself. Aries: the self-created, driven to self-create by taking from outside the known. By your own will you have taken it.
TAURUS. Money. You adapt because you need to.
GEMINI. Communication on the throat chakra level. Your inward voice is your Voice/voice.
CANCER. In the most deserted place you find an oasis. *If there's nothing, you'll find what you need anyway.*
LEO. How you take care of yourself, express your needs; *a serious shift from how you've lived.*

VIRGO. An earnest desire for liberation from work, *or the way you've worked.*

LIBRA. Upper chakras. Stagnation, something that has to change dramatically will melt through.

SCORPIO. Sex, death and money. You have potent male energy. Intense. It's right across from your Aries.

MERCURY. Is in Sagittarius. Learning about the lower orders of consciousness from the higher order. The infinity sign and the medicinal sign are in Sagittarius.

CAPRICORN. House of fame, public relations. Big accomplishment ability. Large possibilities. A magic carpet. Dreamworld stuff.

AQUARIUS. Hopes and aspirations. "Wave of bliss" tsunami here. Letting all areas of yourself flow to get there.

PISCES. House of Karma. Balanced energy.

Last card. You've regenerated completely. Survival despite all obstacles. If there are obstacles, you don't see them. A break-through will permanently alter where you've come from and where you're going.

Your path will merge with people who have been in your life, and whom you are about to encounter, from earlier lives. Finding change through somebody else. Now into sensual bliss—the rose garden.

Asylum card. Recuperation from the life you've led and freedom from worldly concerns. Unbridled care for yourself. This card is about karmic debt come due.

This is a reading of total movement. Your tools and your body are in preparation.

Summation:

Karma—going to be deferred.

You will encounter past-life person.

You will find a path of ecstasy with or through them.

March 26, 1995

Weakness of legs. Weakness of body. Very low energy. Mind

O.K. Brain energy O.K. Body energy weak although a little better today. Slight headaches every day. Due to bright light? Glare?

"Even though I'm going away today, please feel free to call me any time during the week. I will be here next week every day, all week."

Skirt below knees, slit to left side. Small gold heart hanging over shirt top on thin gold chain.

"I'm the only senior acupuncturist chosen from this area to go to the National Commission for the Certification of Acupuncturists Quarterly Meeting. I'm planning take pictures. They've reserved a room in the hotel for me. In Nashville." She pauses and gives Doris a long look.

"You know what the NCCA is?"

"Yes. Yes of course I do."

"I'm leaving on an airplane at 8:00. It will arrive there at 11:30"—she giggles—"the middle of the night!"

"You are honored! Congratulations."

"Thank you! Sorry about what happened before. It was crazy in here, just crazy." She curves her lips to say the word crazy, they're pursed to get out the "C" and the "R." "I'm sorry I didn't have your herbs ready, and you had to come back for them."

She shakes her head, but her expression has barely changed from a smiling flirtatious look to the serious knitbrowed face. Head angled downwards, she looks at the floor, focuses her eyes on it.

March 29, 1995

"Energy much better now?"

"A little better each day. But still not great. How was your trip to Nashville?"

"Very good." As an aside to herself, "but the people there not friendly like here. Maybe they don't like Chinese—I was only Chinese at meetings."

Yes, Doris thinks. *Here, you are used to being adored, but not everyone will adore you.* Aloud she says, "Hongwei, I want to ask you about my herbs. When you are prescribing herbs by the five element system, using the Mother-Child relationship of the organs, are you tonifying the liver, the mother, to strengthen the child, the heart—the next organ in the order of the system?"

"No, not always. Don't always use five element system. Look," she starts to draw Doris a picture of the five elements, drawing the circle in ink on a yellow slip of paper. Instead of "soil" she writes the word "Soul" by mistake.

Then she says "Come sit down." They sit together bent over the paper and, just then, Jeanette appears and says "Carol" or "Jackie" is here.

Doris is left with a piece of yellow paper with the word "Soul" in place of "soil."

In Chinese medicine, the season that soil represents is late summer/early fall, Doris's most depressed, downward time of year.

The next time Doris sees Hongwei there is barely time to talk and she is businesslike and brusque. The office is buzzing; everyone wants her to step into the doorway of their examining room and say how *are* you with her dazzling smile.

Doris hopes for an answer about the Chinese five element system in which the mother or child is used to tonify or sedate. She wants to connect her knowledge about Chinese herbs with the way Hongwei thinks and prescribes. When Doris asks if Hongwei has studied Taoism and the answer is no, Doris still has the desire to know Hongwei's mind. Her Chinese Medicine teachers have spent years studying Taoism and constantly couch their teachings in Taoist phrases and attitudes. She is interested only in their knowledge. Her interest in Hongwei is a desire for depth, for a total knowing of this woman's mystery. Which she knows she can't really fathom. She will continue, nevertheless, to send her signal, her sonar beam towards Hongwei.

"No, I have never studied Taoism," replies Hongwei.

"Hongwei, I think sometimes Taoism was invented by men for the benefit of men. What do you think?"

Hongwei looks questioningly at Doris and shakes her head. She says she doesn't know.

"Maybe the Chinese Communists prevented the study of Taoism while you were growing up and studying in Shanghai," suggests Doris. Hongwei seems to have totally missed even the references to Taoism. Ironic that Doris, an American, knows more about Taoism than Hongwei, who is Chinese.

Rereading her notes, Doris finds the following:

Deficiency of both Spleen and Heart result in insufficient blood since the spleen is the chief organ involved in the production of blood. These deficiencies result in the corresponding deficiency of the amount of heart blood necessary to anchor the shen, resulting in restlessness of the spirit and, thus, insomnia.

Heart yin deficiency includes that of heart blood because yin embodies blood. In heart blood deficiency the person will find it difficult to fall asleep, but once asleep will stay asleep. In heart yin deficiency, the person will find it difficult to fall asleep and will wake up many times during the night. Heart yin deficiency is often accompanied or caused by kidney yin deficiency. Since heart yin loses the nourishment and cooling effect of kidney yin, this leads to flaring up of empty heat of the heart. Heart yin deficiency can also arise after an attack of exterior heat consuming body fluids and exhausting the yin of the heart.

Yin deficiency and blazing of fire is caused by insufficient kidney yin, resulting in a lack of yin to counterbalance heart fire. When kidney yin is deficient, there is not enough water (kidney yin) to control fire (heart yang). Heart fire then blazes upward and disturbs the spirit. Heart and kidneys must be in balance as they represent the two fundamental poles of yin and yang, fire and water.

Heart yang descends to warm and nourish kidney yin; kidney yin ascends to nourish the heart yang. If kidney yin is deficient, it cannot rise to nourish heart yin, leading to hyperactivity of heart fire, or water not controlling fire.

"My heart blood is deficient because my heart fire dries up the yin. Not enough moisture. You can tell this from my pulses, Hongwei?"

"Say again," she says.

Doris says it again.

"You have had this from the beginning." Her legs and feet are twitching with impatience; as she sits, her feet are in and out of her shoes. Her mask shifts.

She explains to Doris, "If your emotions and sleep get better, your breast get better." With one hand she circles her own breast then cups it with her other hand to make a point. Posing for Doris in this way, her head in profile, and jutting out her breast, Doris imagines Hongwei as a woman meant for women. That that's what she's showing Doris.

March 27, 1995

Doris knows that Hongwei has a husband and daughter, although the only thing Hongwei ever mentions about her husband is that whenever their daughter didn't want to practice her piano lessons, he took chopsticks and beat her hard on her knuckles to force her to practice. This translates to Doris as sadistic behavior. Hongwei chose this detail to reveal something about her husband to Doris, but Doris doesn't know if it is to tell her she thinks it's important for her daughter to play the piano, to be disciplined, or to obey her parents. Or that physical and mental cruelty are perfectly acceptable.

But from the way Hongwei tells her the story, from her expression and voice, Doris doesn't think she liked the beatings and wants Doris's reaction to them. But all Doris says is "Really?" which is her usual response when she knows it will take her a while to absorb what she has just heard.

Despite the existence of a husband, Hongwei is the first person Doris has desired in years, the only one she has desired in this particular way. And she has never before chosen someone quite so out of reach. This is the first time in her adult life that she has been attracted to a seemingly straight woman. Right now she thinks her instincts are pretty infallible. Which means that somewhere, somehow, Hongwei isn't straight. She thinks maybe what she wants is someone out of reach. Often, Hongwei does not seem to her like a real person.

But she wants to say: "Hongwei, your office number, 1201, is the same number as my apartment number for 13 years; you are an important part of my recovery. I need the experience of making up herbal prescriptions. It will help me with my studies. I can do Wednesdays after one o'clock."

Of course she will say no; she will refuse to allow Doris to work for nothing. Or to work at all.

The tiny nose, the curved nostrils, the heavy-lidded eyes and tan skin. The full lips and downcast eyes.

March 30, 1995

On some days she nearly rips Doris's watch off her wrist. Or roughly unbuttons her blouse cuff and indicates that Doris should remove her watch by brusquely pointing. Won't touch her or take her pulses until Doris, who is never fast enough, removes her watch. Sometimes, Hongwei lingers for a long time on Doris's breasts, longer than ever before. She says, "I think it is broke; the smaller mass is broke; the herbs are working." She's nodding and smiling.

Doris knows the herbs are working. She also knows that she still has liver blood and liver qi stagnation, a condition that creates breast masses. And she knows now how this condition has come about.

One day Hongwei says, "Since I know your case so well, you need to come only once every two weeks instead of once every week." Hongwei stops. She looks at Doris to see the effect of her words. Doris is impassive. She reminds herself that this is standard practice in herbal and acupuncture treatments. That in most cases, after three months, sometimes sooner, patient visits are automatically reduced.

Doris doesn't answer right away.

"I'll miss you." She gives Doris one of her charming smiles.

"But I'm not the kind of doctor who makes people come for a long time when don't need."

"Whatever you think, Hongwei." Doris tells herself she is prepared for whatever Hongwei offers. That something in her has detached itself from depending too closely on anyone for anything. At the same time she feels her shen has suddenly lost energy.

Doris thinks that most people see her as non-sexual, not sexually viable, although she thinks of herself as both. She has noticed that women in Manhattan, whom she deems attractive, pay a lot more attention to her than they do anywhere else.

I would gladly make love with Hongwei or anyone reasonable who wants me, Doris has thought, without stopping to define reasonable. She will when the time comes. It has occurred to her that paying someone would be easiest. She knows there are women who provide sexual services for women.

More than anyone—Hongwei, as she now knows her—seems the most inconceivable of lovers.

"Hongwei," she ventures, "I would like to have the experience of putting herbal prescriptions together. For my studies. Once a week, maybe, for a couple of hours. May I work with the herbs here?"

"I don't have that many patients who still take raw herbs like you," Hongwei answers. "Not enough for you to come in once every week. But you can start right now. Here is a prescription to fill for six bags." She sticks a yellow slip against the side of the closet door, on it a list of Chinese herbs in *pinyin,* or transliter-ated-into-English names.

While Doris works, Hongwei sits at her desk and pretends to shuffle papers around—telephone message slips. She wants Doris's opinion about why her assistant Jeanette is leaving on a day's notice.

She is very much upset about being left in this way.

Jeanette has told Doris the story immediately on her arrival in the waiting room.

"Jeanette is leaving because now you have cut her hours after you told her last year that you would want her to stay and work full-time when your practice increased. You have taken away her hours so you don't have to pay her benefits, and behind her back you hire another woman, also part-time, to avoid paying benefits for either one. Jeanette is loyal; she cares about you; she will stay with you. Such people are hard to find. Hongwei, you are foolish."

"I work so hard all the time; I don't have time to rest. I can't afford to pay anyone full-time. I don't have money. Why you think she is leaving me? She tell you?"

"She is loyal to you; you aren't loyal to her. Her shen is injured. She cannot stay because she is hurt by what you do. Her shen is injured."

Doris looks at Hongwei; Hongwei looks back and doesn't directly reply. Jeanette is worth the money, Doris insists. And Hongwei insists that she cannot afford to pay a full-time worker; she doesn't have the money.

"In China, people take many jobs, sometimes two or three. People here don't work as hard as in China. She can get another job and work for me, too."

"No, the point is, she is hurt by this decision you have made, so she cannot stay. Her spirit, her shen is hurt. You don't see what I am saying? You don't understand what she is feeling?"

As Doris speaks, she is weighing the herbs by the amount of grams on the scale and putting them in small piles on the tops of the magazine covers. When she can't make out the jar labels, Hongwei points them out for her. She is bending and straightening, bending and straightening, weighing, adding a little, removing a little, standing on her toes. It is very hard work.

"When you finish that one, I have another one for you," Hongwei offers. She gets up and carries over several large packages of herbs that have to be opened and poured into jars. Two hours have passed; Doris can barely catch her breath, and it has gotten late.

"She is depressed. She suffers from low self-esteem. Sometimes she comes to work and cries in front of patients. She is on Prozac for her depression. She tell me her father is same way, very depressed. Her mother want divorce her father. He came to me for herbs."

When she says the words "divorce her father," Hongwei, who has been looking directly at Doris, suddenly drops her eyes to the floor, deliberately looking away from Doris. Doris looks at her questioningly; she does not return the look.

"Hongwei, you don't want to pay her benefits, that is why you cut her hours. Your patients like her. She is intelligent and well-educated. She brings in research articles on acupuncture to show patients. She is good with people."

"I don't understand why she is leaving. I want her stay."

Doris feels exasperated. To change the subject, she asks Hongwei when her birthday is.

"Why you want to know. Are you fortune teller?"

"Just curious. Maybe you and I have the same birthday."

"December 29."

"Oh, the sign of Capricorn. That means you are good at marketing yourself."

"No, I am very bad at marketing myself."

"Hongwei, you know, you could suffer burnout if you work too hard."

"What is burnout? Is that the same as wearing out?"

"Yes."

"I'm very lucky, in this country. Many people have helped me. Since I came to United States I have many American friends. I have no Chinese friends. I have never been to Chinatown."

April 2, 1995
A phonecall between Doris and Hongwei.

Hong Wei: "I have your file out on my desk, ready to call you and you call me!" She pronounces the word file as "feel." Doris notes this with pleasure.

Doris: "It is beautiful clear weather, a lovely time of year, early Spring."

Hongwei: "I don't like the city. I have always lived in the country. I love flowers, animals, the simple life. We are planting dogwood trees near our house, pear trees. Even in China I always live in suburbs. The city, Shanghai, was too noisy for me. We plant two magnolias—big flower trees, in back yard, and one cherry tree. Do you know about dogwood trees? Pear trees?"

For reasons she has never understood, Doris often says the opposite of what she means, especially if it is something she feels deeply about. She hears herself saying she loves the city. "I am a city person; I don't know the names of flowers," when in fact she has been thinking constantly about plants, seeds and pollination. That within herself she feels an upwards moving, something she has felt from almost her first encounter with Hongwei, something she didn't think she could explain so Hongwei would understand or want to hear.

"It would be good for you to find a place, make tiny garden for yourself. You need to plant flowers, take care of them. You need relax. Now in Spring is time to plant. You feel too much stress, too much pressure. Related to central nervous system. Too much stress create breast problems. You need be with trees and flowers. I want you make garden. Nature will take you away from thinking about your nodule. I want you do this."

Doris's mind races. For some reason she is catapulted into her inability to say who she is. Her inner chaos, the element most necessary for her transformation, overwhelms her. The simple words, "I love plants too. I have a garden. I can't stand noise either. 'Yes' to everything you have described; we are alike," remain unsaid.

April 3

My archetypal experience: to come out of a tunnel into the light or darkness in a moving train. Meet the Potnia Theron and feel that buzz all around me when I make contact. Be thrown off balance by that energy. Reel. Not hear half of what is said to me. Fight to keep my balance.

April 5, 1995
   K. says:
   Your grief is real, but you don't have to define yourself by it.
   Your fear is real but you don't have to define yourself by it.
   More than anything else in the world, it is important to you
   to be real.

April 5, 1995
   Paging through an architectural study of Beijing, the imperial
city. Formidable symmetry. Beijing is designed to break down the
will. Nothing grows there; there is nothing organic to break the
strict symmetry of the city. The river is the only element that
comforts. Fluid. Soft.

      My attraction to the word *sacred* is that it is about ecstasy.
      My attraction to the word *secular* is that it is not sacred.

May 10, 1995
   I was careful to tell S., who is inside one of the examining
rooms, pierced with Hongwei's needles for his knee stiffness, that
she is a happily married woman—the happily is the part I don't
actually know—with a daughter. Nevertheless, he told me he fell in
love with her instantly—as he knew he would, he said. Which is
more than I knew when first I entered her office and smelled with
my soul her incredible Metal energy. Heard that metal voice.
   Metal, the element closely related to the Lungs and Large
Intestine organ pair.
   The metal personality can be possessive and domineering when
it is in a state of imbalance. A common state.
   Eros Hosiery Company, a name on the side of a passing truck,
flashes by as the bus engine revs up deep for its climb at top
speed through the Speedway. My picture of Hongwei revs up at
exactly the same tempo. Under her white coat, in a flash, her
clothes are off, her warm skin bare, her pubic hair sparse and
black against her skin, her legs long? short? with well-developed
calf muscles. Her head tilts back as in my red jacket I turn towards
her. Red for fire.

Of course I don't want to see S. in this setting although I'm the one who sent him here for his knee problems. To see him here would be to know his feelings are somewhat like mine, that he is possessed not with sweetness, not love, but a feeling that is near intoxication. Hongwei comes out and says to me, "Your friend S. is here. If you want wait for him just few minutes, he'll be out." I quickly leave.

May 14

Watch a taboo break and it speaks to the taboo events of your own life. I admire artists with the guts to address their own demons. There is no known way to talk to demons and sometimes you get it wrong.

—C. Carr (*The Village Voice,* from a review)

May 17

HW: "Always you are very busy Doris. That is good."

Hongwei loves being admired, even loved by the likes of me. Even though it's proscribed and from a distance. It works enough. For me who has been dry for a long time to find myself wet. Wet for her, wet for the plants and animals of life; wet, just wet.

May 20

Food is longing.

Bagels and creamcheese.

The couple beg. Just say it's O.K., that we can have bagels and creamcheese one time, give us your approval, say it's O.K. just one time.

Five years go by. He still does not give his approval. When the five years are up he says, look, you're nearly 80 years old. Go ahead and do it if you want. But you know I can't give my approval. You know it will harm you.

But still they wanted him to take the responsibility to say they could do it. Which he wouldn't.

It went on in this way.

Food is longing. I am going to the Acme to buy salt and ginger root—not to eat. No. Nothing to eat there.

I ate bagels and creamcheese for breakfast even after I was twenty-five years old. It tasted thick, unpleasant, too much sameness. Too white. Still, it was familiar, I stuck with them. Stuck, yes stuck. My edemic face in the mirror.

Iris spoke. For four years at work I ate my food every day and I didn't say nothing. And this man, very arrogant, talked and talked at me. And I didn't say nothing, I just ate my food.

Because he was this arrogant type I knew if I spoke he wouldn't hear me. So finally, after four years he began to order from SuWen, the macrobiotic restaurant. Everybody at work was ordering from SuWen, so he did too.

Then he said, "See Iris, what you made me do, you made me become macrobiotic."

And I never said a single word to him, I just ate my food. Four years.

The Reiki Master.

Longing. That gone feeling Sonia's hands create. Barely conscious (knowing I'm not, but just barely knowing). Swimming in ether. Floating. Better, I imagine, far greater in depth and scope than dope, LSD, any actual substance.

Her ability to let me let go.

When I was a dance critic and sometimes used the word "gone" about the place some dancer on stage would go, my editor always cut out the word. Thought it was a typo.

What is *gone?*

It is night. My actions are to plant and water.

My actions are to dig.

I am on the train. The place blurs up in my feelings. It is a feeling and it is located in a place. The place is on Eleventh Street between 5th and 6th. An old building. I lived there once in a fifth-floor walkup—or was it the sixth? A tiny apartment, freezing in winter, bathroom down the hall and around the corner. I shared it with another person, a painter named—Ira? Ernie? Fred?

He painted his walls yellow, the ceiling orange, the floor black. I remember circles of black dots. A Van Gogh night sky effect. Mostly I urinated into my sink.

Food is longing. Bagels and creamcheese. For so long I ate them even after I was twenty-five while everyone else drank coffee. Ate them for breakfast. Ate them in a daze of milkiness. Still at the breast in my own way. Unfitting even then.

Going to the Acme for salt, ginger root. Not to eat, no.

Salt for hot water in which to soak my feet to bring the energy down from my head.

Ginger Root. Grate until you have ginger the size of a golf ball. Put the ball inside a cotton cloth. Tie the cloth with a string. Tight. Heat in water but don't boil. Make a compress to strengthen the kidneys.

Two remedies: macrobiotic.

Nothing to do with food.

May 26

BRAILLE

I'm not blind
but I can't see either
Perhaps
that is why
I've always worshiped the body. Not my own,
someone else,
laid my self down
to serve them, glued
myself to their cells to
their heartbeat, listened
with my body entire to
theirs, waited for them,
anticipated their every move
I was their earth, their sun, their water.
waited for them
their best dance partner

May 29

I arrive on Wednesday. At once she comes into the room and announces that today she's going to give me acupuncture to open the channels because, she says, they need to be opened every so often.

Although this is not true, I acquiesce. I've noticed that it is difficult and awkward for her to touch people. I have to laugh at myself at the choices I make.

I lie on the table waiting for her and her needles, thinking of L. who was a good-looking, even magnetic woman who hated to put herself out to touch anyone. The world was meant to lay itself at her feet. Do her. She screamed at the top of her lungs when she came, a piercing scream. Two years doing this. What a conundrum for me to have chosen a person like this when I am myself craving the comfort of flesh, wanting to be held, stroked, loved, understood. That was it—understood. That was what all those strokings and touchings meant; to be loved meant to me to be understood. And that was everything.

Hongwei tells me she will use the new technique of line acupuncture instead of point acupuncture. L-I-N-E. She spells it for me as I inquire further. You thread the needle into the skin in a line.

"I'm thinking of giving a lecture on it," she says. "But a lecture requires too much energy."

She pauses. I understand. She has none to spare. I understand her partially, reaching where I can reach. I hear her explain that she's working at her outermost limits.

She puts the needles in near my wrists, and in both forearms and feet at the ankles, the source points of the meridians.

Asks me before that how my lower back is.

My back is sore from my Yoga class yesterday.

"In two months I have to give lecture on acupuncture at Yoga Society. Will you come and be person I demonstrate on for people in audience?"

"On what day of the week is it?"

"A Sunday."

"What is the date?"

She pauses.

"On what part of the body will you do the needling?"

"Just hands."

She gives a small laugh. "No, you not right person for this. You very private. Like me. You don't want everyone look at you. You just like me. I understand." She is smiling at me and shaking her head.

"Show me where pain is." To my surprise, she touches my lower back, putting both of her hands there, then feels the temperature of my hand, then feels my breasts to see the changes in the lump.

It has changed, but it hasn't shrunk much, although it is softer than it's been. And smaller.

She feels it carefully, then goes on to do the needling.

She says nothing.

I close my eyes with the insertion of each needle, this time very soberly. She can't see my face; she is looking down at the needles; the only reason I feel free enough to close my eyes with her standing over me.

May 31, 1995

This is the last time that I do this.

Mama: The Shrine

Every scientific study on longevity indicates that undereating extends the life span of living creatures. People who undereat, or eat moderately, live longer and get more done.

But MIT studies by Scrimshaw show that given the opportunity, people will exceed their protein, fat and carbohydrate requirements by more than they can possibly utilize

The desire to overeat is the desire to blunt consciousness. Overeating gives the feeling of satisfaction, a certain high for a few minutes before the anger and depression hit when the food reaches the liver. The origin of overconsumption is the desire of people to make themselves feel heavier and more grounded.

The spin, the constant charge of information created by a technological society fragments us. To compensate for this lost feeling we want mothering. Nurturing. Comfort. Want Mama.

Mama.

The same word in every language.

Wanting to feel connected to the earth, we overeat to have that feeling of wholeness. For minutes. Everywhere, the culture's imagery of excess glows; excess we are taught to want by our emptiness, fragmentation, our absence of feeling home.

Chinese Medicine, specifically The School of Attacking and Purging (12th Century A.D.) tells us that the over-stimulation that exists today—too much activity and too much arousal—is too much emotional input and challenge. They say the internal pathology, the root causes of chronic disease are emotional first and intellectual second. The third, however, stems from poor diet and habits of irregular eating and chewing which create too much stress in the digestive system. So wrote Liu Wan Se (1120-1200 A.D.)

The cooling down of both external and internal aspects would relax the person, allow time for them to contemplate.

If people can learn temperance, so that emotion is not overrid-

80

ing their lives, they can pause, reflect, make changes in their lives. Not return to the same lifestyle that made them sick.

Stomach fire is internalized heat, the result of too much emotion and activity and the ingestion of spicy, deep fried, roasted foods or foods baked at too-hot temperatures, and convenience foods. This excess, which makes people crave quarts of cool water, which only adds dampness to the fire—damp heat to the stomach—and cools the fire but briefly.

The stomach, continued Liu Wan Se, is the root of feelings, the emotional aspect, the ability to feel. It is the stomach that gives us the gamut of possible feelings. The stomach starts it all. And stomach fire is the root of our emotional/mental discrepancies.

For healing, Chinese Medicine tells us, the first task is to strengthen the spirit, the shen. If the person has a strong shen, it means their cellular consciousness is good and they can be cured easily because cellular changes come from the manipulation of the body by the spirit. The home of the shen is the heart; if you build up the heart you strengthen the spirit. The shen directs the qi, tells it how to heal you, how to do its work. The shen is embedded in our essence together with the RNA and DNA. In our cells, our bone marrow. For most people to heal themselves, nurturing the spirit is first; the rest will follow. On the other hand, if the healing is too quick, there is often a degeneration into former patterns.

Healing—it does not say this in Chinese Medicine manuals—has to take place between equals so there is a continual exchange of power.

*   *   *

She felt a knot in her chest like she hadn't felt in a long time. It was a week past the first-year anniversary of her mother's death. One week. Although she had made elaborate plans to mark the day, Doris discovered, as the day went on, that she seemed to be avoiding all of them.

She had planned to pick fresh flowers and put them in a vase on her mother's antique bureau, the one on which she had placed photos and mementos, an altar, really, a shaman's *mesa*, a symbolic zoning of power objects on her mother's shrine that she had set up when she had moved into the house.

This is my home. My mother, my father, my sisters, my brother. These rooms. These artifacts that choke and soothe me. My father's painted plates carved in silence under the only light in the room, the warm lamp, his hands curving and cutting his knife through the soft wood, carving out sections so you could see through the designs to the other side. The other side. The weight of his thoughts cutting through wood. No, no thoughts. Carving. His family name, first discovered by him in a 15th century Spanish manuscript in the Bibliotheque Nationale. Sephardic Jew. Destined to wander.

Despite everything I must find a way to claim it for myself, to accept it as mine, to care for it, to love it.

There is no other life for me.

She was going to light one of the 24-hour candles she had bought, the long, thick kind that comes in its own glass jar, and place it next to her parents' antique candlestick holders that stood in the middle of the elegant copper tray in its place on top of the bureau. The tray she remembered being wiped with a soft rag every time her mother's house was cleaned. Just above the bureau, in place of a matching mirror, stood a tall framed picture, a striking frontal self-portrait of Frida Kahlo from the waist up, standing with two white doves perched on her shoulders and two more that she held in her arms. When Doris had first seen the poster she'd known it instantly as the Mistress of the Animals, *the Potnia Theron,* an ikon central to her being. In her gut, known. Dazzling to her still.

Kahlo stood, at what seemed to be the height of her powers, holding a lit cigarette between two fingers, gazing directly through your eyes into your soul. Doris could feel resonate the richness of Kahlo's grief, the depth of her womanly power. She knew the picture was the sacred form, the goddess. Like the photographs of her mother and herself were sacred. Like the old white frame house which stood behind her in the photograph as she stood posing in her sunsuit at the age of three years was sacred.

From the tightly pulled-back braid of her hair that was parted in the center, to her brown legs, and feet encased in worn white-rimmed navy sneakers carefully laced and tied by hands that seemed to be just outside the photo, she was uncomplicatedly happy, loved, a dweller in the Garden of Eden. So it seemed.

Propped against the wall to the left of the Kahlo picture was a small framed photo of her mother at the age of twenty, the sun all over her as she sat smiling on the grass, a pencil to her lips for the poems she would often read and sometimes write, a cape thrown lightly but carefully over her shoulders, looking prettier and happier than she would look ever again.

To the right of the Kahlo picture, resting against the wall, was a piece of brown cardboard on which two photographs were glued, one a picture of Doris at the age of five, standing in a sunsuit in front of the old summer house in New Brunswick. She was smiling, showing her deep dimples. Glued to the right side of the cardboard was a photograph of her mother taken forty-five years later, wearing shorts and a short-sleeved blouse, standing near a deck chair outside the Martha's Vineyard guest house where her parents spent the first two weeks of July for nearly twenty years. Hands thrust uncharacteristically into her pockets, her mother looked happy, almost carefree.

In my recurring dream all my suitcases were packed. It was time to leave to catch the train but I couldn't find my bags. I roamed the cavernous rooms of a house that was lit by many strange lights which cast deep shadows. I looked for the bags without success. I missed the train and awakened knowing I had missed the train again, the same one I had always missed.

After my sickness had passed, the dream disappeared.

On the piece of cardboard, between the two photos, Doris had written the following in her most casual script:

(1) Happiness appears in photographs as momentary, a smile that blots out the rest of the scenery. The look that tells nothing about what came before or after. Why is smiling so necessary to photographs; why isn't frowning?

(2) I look at the photographs of my mother hearing the words "You look like your mother" as "You are like your mother." As if hearing the words would make them true.

Since so many people feel inclined to say them, I wonder if they are true and whether it matters. And, if the first is true, is the second?

The photographs were glued to the cardboard, the words roaming their way around the pictures as a framing device, an assignment she had given to one of her creative process classes. *Find two photographs, glue them against the same background, and write something about them that will connect them.* She had done that assignment herself and placed it where she could see it easily when she wanted. Even a casual glance in its direction told her its energy field was for her a depth charge.

Other things she had placed on the copper tray were three shot glasses in a row, one of which held a tablespoon of uncooked rice. Another was half-filled with water. A third held a teaspoon of salt. They stood before the pictures of Frida Kahlo and Doris's mother (which, oddly, translated one into the other), offerings, to keep her mother's spirit from feeling hunger or thirst.

She had been dreading the day of the anniversary, uncomfortable in her skin about it because she knew she expected something of herself that day, something decidedly more than usual, although she didn't know exactly what.

Yet when the day arrived, she found herself too busy to stop and pay her respects, gather flowers, or to think even randomly about her mother's death.

Instead, she made an appointment to see a famous woman Japanese shiatsu practitioner who was in town, visiting for one day only. The woman would give her a shiatsu treatment and, during the course of that treatment, by feeling the shape and condition of her organs and tissues, be able to tell her not only what was wrong, but what she needed to do to heal what was out of balance.

She had inherited her father's sketchbooks by default by just removing them from his closet after his death. No one cared; no one else wanted them. She was the only one in the family who could read French.

They were filled with drawings: horned figures, faces or whole bodies half-animal, half-human, portraits that were in some way twisted or filled with rage. All out of balance, all in some way thrusting their twistedness into your eye like nightmares. Drawn with great skill and intensity, the shading perfect, each a small masterpiece. Interleaved among the drawings were lengthy poems and prose poems in French none of which she could bear to read. "La Vie, Quel Cauchemar!" was the single phrase she recalled seeing written, extra dark, as she paged through the books. An inexplicable feeling of dread went through her whenever she picked up the heavy journals, which was seldom. Dread at knowing something she wasn't given permission to know. Knowledge she did not want. Yet she could not throw any of the books away. They were, somehow or other, hers. Hers to dread.

Sometimes, deliberately, she would sit down, face the altar, and visualise her mother's face, which was usually laughing as if she had just told a funny story or smiling as if she had just heard one.

Then she would begin to talk to her mother.

Today she avoided doing it altogether. She could not recall, suddenly, what it was she usually spoke about.

Sometimes when she spoke it was in a whisper, in some kind of trance, certain that her mother could hear and understand her. And, when she spoke, looking towards the shrine, her gaze took in everything at once: the skull of a small animal, a fox perhaps, hung with feathers which she had bought in New Mexico; a photograph of herself taken five years earlier with Anna, her five-year-old niece, who wore the woven Mexican dress she had bought the child as a gift. She, herself, was wearing a T-shirt she had purchased in the same market in New Mexico, woven of the same design, in the identical colors.

Posed with their arms around each other, there was something about the two of them in the photograph—brilliant like a deeply cut bas-relief—that was for Doris continually arresting.

Neither had known what the other would be wearing on the day of that particular visit, which was the last time they would see each other until the day of her mother's funeral ten years later.

Then there was a photo of Doris standing in the University Museum, at some celebratory event, with her left arm hooked into the arm of the famous ninety-three-year-old scholar of Middle Eastern prehistory who was holding a glass of wine in one hand, an *hors d'oeuvre* in the other. Her right arm was linked into the left arm of the Chair of the Board of Trustees, a tall outgoing woman she had never liked but whom she thought the world regarded as successful, who died of cancer a few years after the photo was taken.

It was no coincidence that the people on either side of her were dead. When she had placed the photograph on her mother's shrine they had both been alive. What resonance they had for her was that she had been photographed with them and that she was still alive while they were dead. There seemed no other reason for the location, the presence of that photograph on this altar. Now they were shades, guides for her, both of them smiling, half in this world, half in the other.

In the photograph, she too was smiling a hearty smile like a grimace. She was already sick by then and it showed. The pink fleshy cheeks, the slight corpulence, the eyes sunken, the eyelids loose above and below, the heavy dark circles underneath the eyes, the pulses running fast and uneven, the tongue coat yellow and greasy. The need to go home and rest, and, if it were possible, to gather a little strength for the next tasks, which seemed insurmountable. Herself too, half in this world, half in the other.

She picked up the photograph, turned it over, then gazed at the front again.

She could not explain to herself why she wanted to keep it on the altar.

She turned her mind to survey the rest of the objects.

A 20-year-old rolled-up 8 x 10 photo of herself wearing her hair long, clad in a black coat with a bright scarf, taken by a famous photographer who had been a surrealist painter in the 20s, who told her that one day the ability to paint had just "left her." In the photo, Doris's eyes are focused on a place that is either deep in The Underworld or off in the heavens, either one of which she can find whenever she wants to.

Behind her, the scarred walls of the city put the trance of her inward gaze into high relief.

A deep brown antique coat-pin that recalled her childhood.

Youthful photos of her parents: her mother protecting her violin tenderly, against her left side with both hands; her father, seated before a Victrola in his bathrobe, smoking a pipe, his brooding gaze into the camera.

A smudged and wrinkled piece of paper, folded and unfolded many times, on which she had written the farewell speech she had read at the funeral.

The remains of eight or ten blown-out cardboard matches.

An empty, blackened glass that once contained the 24-hour candle the Rabbi had given her to take home after the funeral.

The dried-out, detached label from the same candle on which were printed Hebrew letters she could not read.

A remnant, two inches long, of torn black cloth, with a safety pin, given to her by the Rabbi to wear during the funeral along with the other bereaved members of the family.

A ring of keys from her mother's house to locks that no longer existed, so thick and heavy it felt rich just to let the oily metal lie in her palm.

A delicate cookie tray for which she could not now find practical use.

A rectangle of dusty velvet cloth on which the copper tray rested, which had performed the same function in her mother's house. Except that now, in her house, its function was sacred. In her mother's house it had been sacred in the way ordinary things were sacred because they were markers that never changed, like the seasons.

This time, when Doris visualised her mother, she saw a sad, gaunt face, eyes filled with sorrow, the way her mother had looked during the last two years at the nursing home. As if in a hopeless struggle to engage a single person, a single consciousness which would at least address her by name. As if they knew who she was.

She could suddenly conjure the photograph of her mother at the age of eleven, standing before the orchestra of the Mannes College of Music, just having finished playing the Mendelssohn violin concerto as soloist with them. The picture had hung in the hallway opposite the living room of the family's apartment for years. It continued to be struck by the late afternoon sun with particular radiance. When no one remembered to look at it, her mother passed the photo to the Mannes archive where it stayed on permanent loan.

The photo's moment had burned itself into Doris. Her mother at eleven, small of stature, possessed of perfect pitch, with a passion that needed always to be tempered, stood triumphant before the assemblage of seasoned adults. Her mother had recounted to Doris how her music teacher warned her to control the excess of passion she could too easily pour into her playing.

Famous violinist dies at eleven years old. Buried at Mount Hebron Cemetery, age 91.

The funeral; one year later the unveiling of the stone.

The sister who doesn't speak, who pretends not to know Doris.

Kate

Written in soft, smudgy pencil on an 8 1/2 × 11 sheet, folded in quarters.

Doris dear,

Neither of us won the little game we were playing; I'm glad it's over. You weren't courageous enough to state your intentions and I'm no "grave digger."

Here are the facts:

(1) I'm very fond of you.

(2) I enjoy being with you.

(3) I would do almost anything for you.

Since these are the prerequisites for friendship, what are you waiting for? I think you're aware of my flexibility and are contorting it into a nasty little snare in which to catch you, me or some damn thing. Don't waste our time. In your candid (?) confessions you label yourself "nasty, obnoxious, insipid, etc." I think you are not. If you are trying to make an ass of me don't commend yourself so highly for I am already that to bother about this relationship. You're aware of my sensitivity and triumph in using it as a mechanism to manipulate me. I love you in my perverted little way in spite of your bitchiness so please don't give me a hard time. You are one of the few people I put on a par with myself; you may set up the terms of friendship—if you delight in that. Please allow me to see you alone or in a crowd and don't be afraid of me. I have no desire to hurt you. If you are not interested we can drop the whole thing. If you have guessed that I'm a novice at this sort of thing, you are right. *Si nos yeux n'etaient si bruns, toute ma vie aurait changee.*

Don't be flattered when you read this. That you have so little desire to see me is depressing. May I see you soon?

Kate

Typed, with black ink signature, on 8 1/2 × 11 sheet, folded in half.

Look, Miss Mills, I'm tired of this nonsense! Does it occur to you that I don't "want" you, that if I did "want" you it wouldn't take me one whole year to "get" you? You think I'm shy and inexperienced but you're wrong. I'm neither. I like suave, intellectual women. You're neither. I really don't like to get involved with emotional kids—they take everything too seriously. Because someone looks at you, you don't have to assume they're willing to put up with your emotional quirks. Oh, I like you well enough but I don't take you or anyone else seriously. When we met I told you "friends are a passing commodity" and that still holds. Making love to someone is like buying them a cup of coffee—nothing more. It's nothing to be coy or shy about. You're a nice kid and I don't want to hurt you. Will you please not take what I say or do seriously? I don't have to be coached in such matters. If I have the desire to touch someone, I touch her, she doesn't have to tell me to. For the 500th time, I love you and am in love with you—but that doesn't mean I'll take all the garbage that goes along with it. Nasty letters, fighting, and general chaos are not conducive to any sort of relationship. This isn't to reject you, only to inform you. You know very little about me, so you shouldn't assume things. I know what I want and who can give it to me. I know this situation and its circumstances better than you do. I don't care what you do when you're not with me; anything I do when I'm not with you is none of your business. Don't take this as a personal insult—it's time for you to stop kidding yourself. You're pretty sexy and all that, but hardly the type anyone like me would want to get mixed up with. I've made that point over and over but you refuse to accept it. You pass it over as shyness. You never doubt for one minute you are what everyone wants. You're going to be hurt one of these days and I don't want to be the agent.

Good luck in your endeavors. Get enough sleep, eat enough and take care of yourself. You're going to be a fine woman some day

If there's anything I can do for you, you know where I live.

Don't hate me for this or get upset—it shoudn't be that important. If there's anything I want from you, I'll take it without being asked or prompted. I know myself better than you know me.

> And the hole in the heavens
> brown browed doris soft
> smiles white
> tossing turning
> angel soft
> breaks the night.
>
> Katharine Richmond Fletcher
> 34-33 47 St
> Astoria, NY

In faint pencil on three sheets of two-hole notebook paper, one side of the page.

Dear Doris,

It is difficult to explain the emotions involved.

At our first meeting, your courage was admirable, your spilling milk over me in the cafeteria was an impressive accident. Your offer to replace the milk was laudable, but (as I pointed out) I'd had my fill of milk products for the day. Since then I have learned to penetrate almost any "veneer" you might choose to don—except for oscillating eyes and breasts and vacillating hips. (I naively accepted them in terms of their connotations and denotations.)

I would like to see you alone at my house at your earliest possible convenience or, for that matter, on any other occasion. No prophesy is offered here for my behavior on that or any other date. Since I haven't experienced it, it doesn't exist. Don't consider my rejecting you because once I have accepted someone their essence never leaves me. My sensitivity and sincerity—choosers of my "essences"—make no account for pettiness that might appear. To paraphrase an earlier letter: I enjoy being with you, I would do most anything for you, I'll always love you.

Let me know if there is ever anything I can do for you.

Although material things are all that I can offer, I offer them openly and abundantly.

It is late and my throat is sore from smoking so much. I'm relieved, happy and embarrassed all at the same time. Please attribute any snideness or cynicism to the tired state, the mechanism of defense, or to my loving you so much I don't want to appear an ass. Goodnight little darling. I love you in my passive, meager way.

Sincerely,

Kate

Penciled, the letters filling the spaces between the lines of 6 × 9 three-holed, ripped-out notebook paper.

I'm sorry you're infected with so deep a resentment—"ah me, to think I started this whole thing. Had I but known." There's no need to be. Although you say you are emotionally involved "hardly at all," your emotional spasms indicate otherwise. You shouldn't take these things that seriously, Doris. I would like to say you are unimportant to me, but I would only be kidding myself. I don't mean to be condescending, but you're not the most important thing in the world. If you are so thoroughly disgusted with me, tell me so and don't bother with me. Perhaps I'll "grow up" emotionally and learn to be glib about such matters. At this point, expressing love for the love object does not seem ludicrous. Sorry you had to be the "recipient of my feelings which I choose to pour into you," but you didn't have to be so eager a recipient.

Yes, I can answer what the hell is it that you want without reference to Aristotle. I informed you that I thought you were at least my equal or I wouldn't have bothered with you—that we approached things generally on a different level—the levels being equally valid—and that some kind of communication (letters, conversation) would be profitable to us. We are a far cry from that hypothesis. Attribute this disparity to my ascetic nature or my unadult medium of expression. I've told you, friends are a passing commodity—they always have been. Sorry I can't go outside myself to please you. You are a beautiful entity—physically, intellectually and emotionally. I can't tell you (I don't quite know) why it is you I love, I can only say that if I met someone like you, I would love her as well.

It's unfortunate you mangled the card I sent you with the poem on it and upset yourself. "Little Mills with a dirty neck" merely refers to the way you wear your collars up. As for my "paranoid reflection and refusal of the essence of the human being . . . sex, and sensuality and emotion," at the beginning of your letter you say I "poured" my feelings into you, on two other occasions you were aware that I wanted to make love to you. Does this suggest a rejection of sex? Incidentally, the essence of man is not sex. All animals enjoy sex, the differential between man and animal is rationality. Hence, the essence of man is that he is a rational animal.

How did you deduce that I am an intellectual competitor of yours? A metaphysician knows metaphysics, a poet, poetry. I can find no justification for your rejecting something you know little about—namely Aristotle. Upon your recommendation alone, I borrowed some modern poetry from the library, much of which I enjoyed. You see, I'm not a metaphysical snob; there is much to learn and you have something to offer me. If you held the same attitude, and not that you, at the age of 19, know all there is to know, you would not reject me, Aristotle, and philosophy so indiscriminately.

You have no emotional obligations to me.

The following might be incidental, if not uncalled for. I would never touch you if I knew you didn't want me to. You've made it clear, thank you. I hope you are not angry about this or the last note I sent you. You have a peculiar way of interpreting what I do, say, or write. I'm not malicious. Half the time, I don't know where this relationship rests. If you check my reins, or tell me to check them, it would be conducive to a more pleasant, constructive relationship.

I enjoyed reading the dialogue from your play, although many of the concepts conflict with mine. "This I suppose will go on and I will take gladly what you give to me with no reproaches, complaints or statements. Who am I to complain? Indeed, in any way, at any time or place, anywhere near you, I am lucky and know it."

It's exactly what I want to say to you, Doris.

Sincerely,

Kate

N.B. About the dialogue; of course, I don't know the rest of the play—but what else does Stephen do but love Marianne privately? She says, "Although I love you in a way, you are too private to make it mutual." S. has little reason to share his love with her—she loves him "in a way" and she's "always inaccessible . . . flippant . . . evasive." Love should be secure enough to make game playing and evasion unnecessary. Lovers should know each other well enough to be candid with each other. If she were a realer person (evasion = escaping reality) he would not have to "go away in the corner . . . and marvel at his capacity to love" but could overtly experience it with her. The sex act proper, I should say, is the expression of mutual love—"the only time I felt secure with you was when we were bone to bone. . . ." S. is apparently using it as a device—to enjoy the security of being near M. for a short time. There ought to be more to love than that.

I strongly challenge:

"You need me far more than I need you, for now you can only live, loving those who are older and more flippant than yourself. As you get older you will learn not to be so free with your emotions. . . ."

If you're equating age with maturity, maturity does not equal flippancy, quite the contrary. The embittered old are often cynical; flippancy is found in adolescence. Maturity is the ability to discriminate between the important and the trivial. Flippancy tosses much into the receptacle of triviality. If you were saying that lovers should be flippant—that's your prerogative. I think love should be constructive, not the sublimation of one party at the expense of the other. It should be mutual understanding, sexual desire, etc.

Typed, on a torn-in-half sheet of 8 1/2 × 11 paper, the closing and signature penciled in.

Dear Doris,

From your attitude Fri. in the auditorium, I assumed you were in love with me and desired a sexual relationship. This erroneous assumption, acting on my more sincere love for you, prompted me to assume a sexually aggressive role. Fortunately, this is a passing state. Since you are not in love with me, any relationship of this sort is unnecessary and uncalled for. I'm sorry to have bothered you with these trivialities. I have for you, Doris, all the respect, humbleness and love I am capable of possessing.

Sincerely,

Kate

Typed on a sheet of 8 1/ 2 × 11 three-holed, lined, looseleaf paper, signature omitted.

Pardon my indifference last week, it wasn't anything you did or said, but my realization that our relationship was completely void of any basis. Apparently you have no physical attraction for me. My telling you you are rude was not because I was jealous of your friends but because you were rude. I have little to be jealous of with reference to your clan. Perhaps your friends are charming, intelligent, etc. They're yours not mine. When you assume the role of sorority gal I'm repulsed at us both. I know you are not that or I would not care (this logic is fallacious, but I believe the hypothesis). I am aware that we like each other equally well but this does not oblige us in any way.

My husband Frank is going away to visit his parents on Fri 19. Will you be my guest for the week? Don't be afraid of me, you're the last person I would hurt.

If my behavior is unorthodox, remember you are orthodox in a

social sense, I am not. I seek validity on other levels. Please don't
stop liking me for anything as trivial as that. And please, Doris, if
you won't be my guest, be a frequent visitor.

*   *   *

This is a poem by Sappho:

An Absent Friend

> A glorious goddess in her eyes
> Were you, her comrade, and your songs
> Above all other songs she'd prize.
>
> With Lydian women now she dwells
> Surpassing them, as when day dies
> The rosy-fingered moon excels
>
> The host of stars, and light illumes
> The salt sea and the cornland glows
> With light upon its thousand blooms.
>
> In loveliness the dew spills over
> and with new strength revives the rose,
> Slim grasses and the flowering clover.
>
> But sadly up and down she goes,
> Remembering Atthis, once her lover,
> And in her heart sick longing grows.

I thought you would like it.

*   *   *

*In blue ink on a sheet of 3 × 5 notebook paper, holes on
one side.*

After reading your letter several times I am, again, forcibly
affronted by the significance of this situation for you and me. How
can I evaluate? Temporal duration will offer the lacking hypothesis.
Is it worth the effort and confusion D. can so readily stir in me?
The tiffs in which she is merely saying, "You think I'm stupid but

I'm not." If she knew how I admire her—her intelligence (of a different sort than mine, which, as she vehemently holds, is less extensive on one hand, more on the other), her unique sensitivity. If she could know there is no need to prove it to me! So I observe, do nothing, and accept whatever she offers. Miss Mills, how I love you!

I'm still in the shock of your accumulated gall, "What do you want Kate?" I won't grab you—I'm not that assuming. I enjoyed your "defense mechanism" in explanation of my "defense mechanism." The panacea is "don't bother me Katharine." Do you want to be cured? I don't suspect so, but then again I have a way of projecting. (Is that accurate?) I know what I know—do you? Tell me.

I have beautiful eyes.

Well, pet obsession, seasons greetings.

Typed, on a sheet of 8 1/2 × 11 paper, folded in quarters.

When an old oak sheds its leaves, it rejoices, hoping for a more beautiful dress next season; but when the leaves are torn from a sapling she whimpers, "This has never happened before. Don't leave me;—I'm not eager to learn what spring will bring." She is unheard. She stands stripped, crying for warmth. When spring offers her leaves, she will laugh, for her bark will have become callous. In her nakedness, she will have found clothes. She will learn to play and sway with an evil gale, to find warmth in its coldness. She will not want the silly things she previously loved.

*   *   *

We love not to be loved but to know we can love.

*   *   *

Should one degrade oneself to maintain a balance with another? Or better, fulfill oneself and return to the higher station? Least wise is to assume a high position, for eventually the high will give way

and the teeterboard will send each to her respective axis. Opposites
attract, but they also conflict. The friction brings not warmth but
burns. The scorched may still survive, but charcoal is dead. If the
balance but sways, there may be hope. But hope is useless where
there is not faith.

*   *   *

And the black cloak of memory envelops not.
How the wind of the fleeting hours makes us cold.
Soon to be parted by the wormy sod.
For nebulous death is the omnipotent victor.
There no kindling is nor whom to kindle.
There where we are not and here we dwindle
Into the contagious nothingness we have approached.
Not for a day for there are not such.
There where we knew not what we loved so much.
Thrice crossed or not we meet this fate
Some too easily, some too late.
Why not? Did black death think some too white?
Did she neglect them out of spite?
Come to me then you doris witch
Come save me from what is black as pitch
That does between us come in time.
If we to darkness go—will you not grow as dark as I
Or perhaps no. Foolish me to assume
there is aught beneath a kiss so firm.
Beautiful colors on our canvas we laid.
Why did you not tell me we only played
The game indulged in by all dotes?
Two minds on summers days did play
Two bodies mused in a cold hall way.
Why did you leave me with a mind so sour
To fill the spot where grew your flower?
Come back you fleeting demon
Come back and till your pun

You've twisted my heart and burned my brain
With your approving eyes and your shredded tongue.
Now prepare me for what you have done.
Finish not stop what you have begun.
Let not our bodies of our minds make fun.
Soon we to eternal dark will go
Why do you make it fast not slow?
When I touched your lovely hair
How I wished that I were there
To protect your head from now to then
and brush your cheek now and when.
It is not there—to touch no more
Silly optimist to think you will last
When you are gone, you will be past.
While you are able do not tarry
It will climb up from behind and take you quickly.
Why not venture to compete with time
And perhaps I might your apprentice be
Time cannot claim that which has no name.
Darkness then of a lighter shade
To come between us—our bodies invade.
Then, thrust us in the dust.
For to be thrust? Not so
But lay us low
for our victory we will have won.

I was interested once, if once is eternity.
Katharine Richmond Fletcher
188 55th St.
Astoria

   One year later, Doris's older sister, Sheila, invites her to visit San
Francisco for two weeks. Doris accepts.

*Handwritten in black ink on airmail paper, postmarked July 6
11 p.m.*

Angel baby, I don't know exactly how one writes to you,
particularly how I should write to you. Too much has been said
without employing words to ever, without much difficulty, compose
a letter to you. Tell me everything: how the trip felt, what you
thought, and your present state. For me, today was eventful
indeed. I had lunch with you and started my summer courses.
Tonight I'll love my darling perhaps too desperately for action
because it is not long before she leaves. I still say it is 6,000, not
3,000 miles. I still say I'm surprised you're going on this visit. I
suppose I should be "bigger" but I don't know. School started with
many vows and much humility but I can't vouch for it remaining
on that level. The outcome of the mysticism course will undoubted-
ly include a mystical experience. The other two will tumble along
ordinarily. My energies begin to wane as I start to plan to fulfill my
scholastic obligations within the next weeks.
The objects of thought are in the sensible forms. (*Written in Attic
Greek*.)

July 7, 12:30 a.m.

Precious, upon reading your letter of Wednesday I cried just a
little. Baby I miss you so much. Only ten more days to go. Please
darling don't go away from me anymore. I love you too much to
bear it.

Despite my earnest plans for last night, I didn't accomplish
much. I went to bed at 10 only to get up at 11, back at 11:30.
This went on until about 2.

You are there for 5 1/2 hours, N.Y. time. How does it suit
you—the climate, the people?? Did you sleep on the plane? How
was your take-off, your landing and welcome from Sheila and
Victor? Regards to Sheila. Tell her something from me, anything
she enjoys hearing. Give Victor a big (but not a "Kate's") hug and

squeeze from his "Uncle" Kate. Take care of my precious baby girl and get her back to me safely and as soon as possible.
I love you,
Kate

July 9, 9:30 p.m.

A letter written at your place. As I suspected, the phone nuisance was none other than Bill. We had a good fight over the phone. He kept ringing and ringing. I at first said that this was not the number he wanted. However, and reasonably, he kept ringing and ringing. It was driving me to my wits end. I picked up the phone and told him Doris was not here. He began to scream at me, very rudely and addressed me "Kate." This infuriated me more. He also called me "young lady" and what was the idea of not giving him the information he wanted. I told him I am neither the welfare dept., nor the bureau for missing persons, and indeed not Kate nor Doris to whom he alluded. I asked him who he was, he refused to say, except that he was a very good friend of Doris's—her best friend. When he asked why I wouldn't answer the phone I told him that it was perhaps because I didn't want to talk to him. He asked who I was and if I knew you. I said I had met you only casually through a friend. He asked if the friend was Kate. I said yes. He asked if I had rented or sublet the place from you and when I said yes, about two weeks ago, he said that was a lie because he had come to see you here less than two weeks ago. He asked my name—I gave the name of my school friend Betty Durgin—and refused to leave his. He continued his maniacal raving. I told him I could not hold myself responsible for Doris's petty friendships and social obligations and hung up.

I don't think I'll hear from him again. He was furious and so was I.

I do wish you would pretend you never knew that foolish queen, he's thoroughly unbearable.

12:30 a.m.

It feels strange to be at your house knowing that you will not come or call. The place is messy, a cold, impersonal messiness, things as if undone by a person that is well-loved. I calculate there will be no letter awaiting me today. There will be tomorrow though. This damned paper got stuck in the damned typewriter. I'll write you another letter when I get home. Refrigerator defrosted. Books returned.

I love you.

9 more days.

Kate

July 12, 5:30 p.m. (In faint pencil)

You'd better hurry back. I didn't sleep last night. When I did doze, I kept waking myself up by talking in my sleep. I've scarcely eaten a thing for three days except coffee and cigarettes. One might just as well be dead as to continue like this. This horrible lethargy. What to do? Will next Monday ever come or is it a foolish figment I have constructed to pacify myself? What will you be like when you return? I need your love constantly, darling, every minute, else I could not bear this task. I am much too old (or young or unable) to love at a distance. You must be here, you must be with me and touch and kiss me often, if only to keep me aware and living. You must never, never leave me again, I don't care what the reason.

Seven years later.

Written in ink on the front and back of the program of a Summer Session Classical Concert, The Ars Nova Trio. Rutgers, The State University, Summer Mathematics College Institute.

I hope you did not throw away my first letter because it was not in itself nasty. Just the postcript was, a little.

It is unpleasantly rainy and cold here. I am depressed and chilled and will not go to class this afternoon.

We are having a retaliatory exam Fri. in advanced calculus which will really cut us up or down (whatever that phrase is.) Some fucks complained to the director about the teacher and he's mad as hell and will show us how little we know, etc. I'm sorry I came to this lousy joint and will surely never go to an Institute for Math Teachers again. I miss you very much but now there is nothing I can do about it. Before at least I could jump into La Dauphine and go to you. This lady here (Sandy Burke, pushy) is begging me to quit my job at Angelus College and come to work in her school in Sept. It's a N.J. State Teacher's College, and I'm just the kind of person they're looking for, etc. Actually, it's a very good deal, 30 minutes from Times Square, tenure, state employee, close to Rutgers, and she is persistent. She went so far as to call the head of her department to arrange for an interview but I keep saying no. She's too pushy. It would be an ideal job in a year or two. Then she said I should teach there next summer. She talks so loud and fast I can't get a word in. She's one of those people who "gave up smoking" which really means "gave up buying cigarettes" so she's always taking mine. She insists I go with her to see the campus, she's sure that once I see it I will throw up everything and stay there. (She's married, has 3 kids.) Crazy lady! I should go home to get some clean clothes, I don't have any more left. Maybe I'll just wash out these things and keep wearing them over and over. The whore (Dierdre) disappeared again and no one knows what happened to her. Spicky has removed her rings and goes out drinking every night with different undergrad boys. She's exhausted the ones in the Institute. Homesick indeed! She chuckles, "If they only knew I am married with 2 children, ho ho." She pulls in about 3 every morning. I don't know how she does it and where she gets the energy because she's up at 7 a.m. or earlier. Someone stole Sandy's book ($11) but she keeps saying someone *borrowed* it because she belongs to the SANE Nuclear Committee and CORE and all those organizations which refuse to admit to themselves that there are evil scummy people in the world. She appears to be quite enlightened and kind (but of course you can never tell.) As you can see I'm running out of paper, I want to mail this soon. It's still raining; I'll have to get drenched again. I'll try to call you tonight at 10:00. July 8. Only 5 more weeks.)

*   *   *

Forty-eight

In the pursuit of learning, every day something is acquired.
In the pursuit of Tao, every day something is dropped.

Less and less is done
Until non-action is achieved.
When nothing is done, nothing is left undone.

The world is ruled by letting things take their course.
It cannot be ruled by interfering.

— Tao Te Ching

The Internal Causes of Illness

Emotions are the root of the internal causes of illness and carry inside them a sociology, a social construct. According to the laws of Chinese Medicine, we adapt to the environment by way of our feelings. Illness, which is psychosomatic, carries within itself the signs and symptoms of itself. Internal pathology is the cause of all chronic conditions.

The Seven Emotions

Anger (The element of Wood, the Liver). Wood travels upwards the way trees do; the pressure of blood moves upwards. This person is angry. She suffers chronic headaches and the inability to resolve them. The ascension of anger gives her a red face and eyes, makes her feel superior. Anger is a statement of elevation; she's above other people.

Joy/Happiness/Excitement (The element of Fire, the Heart). Fire scatters the qi whereupon the other emotions get dispersed. It elevates her, gives her a feeling of superiority, excitement. Feeling cherished and expansive, her heart races, she feels palpitations. She doesn't want to sleep, she wants to stay awake and relish the excitement. Happiness creates the inability to fall asleep. Joy wants to hold onto its qi, wants it to last forever. It is hard for her to think of letting it go even to sleep.

In the old days, according to Chinese Medicine, emotion was known, simply, as love. The heart contains the need to know, in life.

Drinking coffee gives her the energy, the pep to take on the questions of the day. The tip of the tongue is the heart of the heart. A tongue which is red at the tip is a sign of longing for the answer she's been consciously pondering for years and can't find sovereignty over. The redness on the tip of the tongue will remain until, through the ingestion of herbs, the spirit is healed or promotes letting the question go.

Pensiveness (The element of Earth, the Spleen). Excessive thinking. Obsession. Sympathy. She slows down her movements to think/obsess/feel for others, as she would put others into her earth, her maternal nature. Sluggishness is a mirror image of the world. The spleen person is like a sponge.

Dampness, a quality that lingers like fog, is characterized by a slowing down of concentration and quickness. Cuts away her ability to see clearly.

Grief (The element of Metal, the Lungs). Depresses both her qi and her ability to live life. It is the feeling of loss, the seeking for compensation. She is told about her social status, belittled. She wants to replace that sadness.

Respiration. The lungs contain the ability to let things in and out and let go of them. The emotion of forgiveness allows her to do this.

Fear (The element of Water, the Kidneys). Waiting suspends the qi. Everything is still.

Two subcategories:

1. *Worry (The elements of Earth, the Spleen, and Metal, the Lungs).* Makes the energy stop because she's concentrating on the anticipation of loss.

2. *Shock or Fright* (*The element Water, the Kidneys*). Disengaged from all emotions she doesn't know what to do.

Wind is the cause of disease, the motivating cause, the force that drives heat, dampness and cold into the body. All disease is an invitation to change, and it is wind that destabilizes and brings about change, is the motivating fire that allows us to change. Animals under stress move around and pace in an effort to find their ease. She avoids going to the zoo, she does not like to see their restlessness.

The direction you're going in can be the root of your illness. Your self in relation to society. The social construct is part of the disease process. Sometimes she thinks of beginning a new life by moving to a new place and not following her old patterns because the people she meets won't be expecting them.

Emotions put us in a certain place. If you take the correct herbs they help find the vector of energy from the physical effects of emotions.

Chinese Medicine doesn't believe passion happens without intentionality—

"Temptation was too strong . . .

"I was overwhelmed with grief . . .

"I lost control. . . ."—despite her belief that emotions are what make her feel alive.

She is struck by this. Everything in her romantic European upbringing is opposed to this statement about intentionality. On pain of death she realizes she must avoid "falling" into a sexual relationship with R. because she sees suddenly there is no such thing as "falling," there is only "deciding" or "going." She has yet to drain her desire as one would drain heat or dampness from the body.

You say to yourself "Is your qi depressed? Is it possible to put your unconscious into a box? Where are you now?

"Angry?"

The idea of the emotions.

All chronic conditions are from internal pathology.

Herbal approaches: The sour taste is an astringent. It calms anger and sedates the external expression of emotions. Sour *zyziphus* (dates) calms the shen, calms insomnia and emotional restlessness. The tranquilized, sedated person is more balanced in her behavior, doesn't show animosity or force us to deal with it. The Chinese Communists wanted you to prove you were a loyal communist. They didn't care whether or not you had anger inside you.

Differing Approaches to Disease
The Confucian. Don't let your emotions "carry you away." The ingesting of ginger and scallions allows you to get rid of wind before it descends into the body. Because emotionality is a force for change it is necessary to extinguish the wind. For this use Unicaria/Gambir or Gastrodia (Cat's Claw) which grows better around parasites. It is good to take when we have something that eats away at us. That lives in us, like parasites. Gastrodia is used for multiple personalities.

In Chinese Medicine, sedatives calm the shen and extinguish wind. They can be used to control you and make you unaware of the reason you have the emotions.

The Buddhist. Alchemical. The alchemical tool is to give (or take) bitter taste which will drive you into the suffering, the emotions, the bitterness of life.

The idea is that life is suffering and suffering, illusion. Moving into the negative allows you to transcend it. Then you are able to move into the positive.

The Behavioral. We characterize people by our observations about them. Consumed with obsessive thinking, the damp person is slow; she hates this quality in herself. Using behavioral modification they tried putting her into a different environment so she could become more like a wood person. A wood person does not want to take on other people's problems. Stimulate the liver and you stimulate wood, whereupon the person begins to express anger and scream at other people. This change changes her environment. New people come around. Old people drop away.

The Constitutional. The only way we can change a person is to build their strength first so they can realize who they are which works well with pyschological problems. The idea is, build the kidneys because the kidneys contain all possibilities; thus, you build the constitution.

The Chinese alchemists took perverse, gross elements like urine, and tried to transform the constitution, to make gold of lead, to get the person to see herself as valuable, precious, healthy. Not diseased.

Alchemy must be done at the right hour on the right day. Minerals build the constitution (salt changes it) though the person might not want to be changed. She may like herself as she is and feel she is the way she wants to be; minerals calm her.

To take something gross and make of it something precious is the tradition of alchemy. To know oneself, the most precious thing one can know, is the alchemical process. The germination of new life from seeds is constitutional therapy. Biota seeds, for instance or lotus seeds.

Seeds probe deep in the body. The original herbalists selected the seeds of plants that grow near water because water is the place of most possibility.

Our suffering provides us with the alchemy, the means to make ourselves different. The Buddha is represented seated on top of a lotus flower; the lotus flower represents metamorphosis.

The seed of the lotus is used for issues that are both psychological and constitutional.

Sexual energy, the essence of the body, the essence of the kidneys that gives birth to us as beings is the water element. Water is the element of possibilities. Water falls into the cup. The cup is willing to contain it.

Water is the root, the mother of existence.

In the Tao, we want to turn back to the nature of the mother. Each breath is connected with the essence of eternity.

Our body is the vehicle by which we express our life. The kidneys grasp the qi, which is breathed in by the lungs, and they anchor the qi. In order to grasp the qi, the breath has to expand into the kidneys.

If we can breathe deeply again, we can return to the mother.

The Triple Heater governs the balance between fire and water. In life, water is below (the kidneys) and fire is above (the heart). The kidneys give us the self—our life's root, what we are born with.

The heart is the ruler, an organ with intelligence and underlying spirit. We become spiritive when we realize the individual we are. The heart, on a quest for something out of life, looks for a challenge. Hopefully, the heart is satisfied at the end. How is it possible for her to become her own ruler? When she becomes satisfied with the path of her life and no longer has a question that needs to be asked.

If the question remains unanswered, perversity enters at the cellular level where it tries to discharge the cellular pathology. The question keeps her awake nights because the heart wants to move towards completion; insomnia is incompleteness.

Heart fire gives her the lesson, the curriculum, what she has to conquer in life. Chinese Medicine says we need to balance ourselves with whatever we're exposed to, and develop a sense of sovereignty over it. Between fire and water should be the sovereignty of water.

Let her sovereignty be water.

The Triple Heater is used in the alchemical tradition to regulate the heat of the three parts of the body; upper, middle and lower.

The way to cook something is to put the fire (our passions) below and the water above. We must take our desires—the fire—and ground them, put the water on top of them.

Lao Tzu said: if everything is possible, why do anything?

Alchemy is the redemption of spirit from matter.

If it is hard to breathe, try the herb *fritillaria*. The kidneys control inhalation. *Fritillaria* strengthens the kidneys' ability to grasp the qi.

In the 12th Century Yuan Dynasty, four great thinkers looked at society. We do too much, they said. People cannot slow down, cannot relax.

Liu Wan Se: The hot condition is a mirror image of our lives. We are like fire burning loose.

Zang Zhe He: People are too active, intemperate in our diets, too yang. We allow our internal problems to persist; we never treat them properly, so they become chronic conditions. It is of utmost importance to maintain the integrity of the inside of the body. The method of the School of Attacking and Purging is to purge through enemas and sweat. To clean, to purify the internal terrain.

Li Dong Yuan: Why is it that people develop chronic conditions? That women develop phlegmy cysts in the breast and elsewhere? Let us look at the entire digestive system. It is because something has failed in the gut.

Li Dong Yuan: We suppress deep within ourselves our unfulfilled passions, aspirations, desires and dreams. He names this dormancy condition "Yin Fire." The feelings and emotions we have consciously suppressed and unconsciously repressed burn up the constitution of the body. Our burning (and always sublimated) passions cause the literal burning out of the internal organs. It is like fire, which creates the conditions of thirsting and wasting. Diabetes for instance.

What we consider to be modern illnesses like HIV, Mononucleosis, Epstein Barr, Chronic Fatigue, Lupus, Li Dong Yuan would say are the result of feelings we have suppressed consciously and repressed unconsciously, the result of Yin Fire.

Zhu Dan Xi: Here is the problem: We are creatures of such habit that once we feel stronger and better we return to the habits that first made us sick. Each day we need to invent something different, to not go back to the old ways, to change.

Yin Fire

It is my mother's voice that I hear, repeating my name to me three times:

Doris

Doris

Doris

A sound of disappointment, a sound tinged with grief underneath the D and the O, the RIS trailing off so that the first two letters are the primary sound, the last three the fermata, the single held note that passes away. At the beginning a muted "Oh," understood, but not heard, before the first *Doris*.

Each time I hear the sound it is said in a tone lower than the one before. A sad sighing sound, a descent.

This is how I reply to my mother in my own voice: *I am wild. I need someone to make a home for me, to care for me, to provide a place for me so I can feel less wild, and then, to let me be wild.*

An incantation.

I repeat it to my mother in my mind.

After a pause, she replies with the same three words: (oh) Doris, Doris, Doris.

The oh behind the words, silent.

Her disappointment. Something in me I can never mend for her. Never fix. Her ultimate sadness about the ways in which I have failed her.

I repeat what I have said.

It is a mantra. My body has known it in its darkest outposts, but has not known how to say it. Until now.

It had happened in Switzerland during the first year of his cure—during the first months, in fact. At the time he was still like an idiot; he could not even speak properly, and sometimes

111

he could not understand what was required of him. One bright, sunny day, he went for a walk in the mountains and walked a long time, tormented by a thought that, try as he might, seemed to be eluding him. Before him was the brilliant sky, below—the lake, and around, the bright horizon, stretching away into infinity. He looked a long time in agony. He remembered how he had stretched out his arms towards that bright and limitless expanse of blue and wept. What tormented him was that he was a complete stranger to all of this. What banquet was it, what grand, everlasting festival, to which he had long felt drawn, always—ever since he was a child, and which he could never join? Every morning the same bright sun rises; every morning there is a rainbow on the waterfall; every evening the highest snowcapped mountain, far, far away, on the very edge of the sky, shows with a purple flame; every tiny "gnat" buzzing round him in the hot sunshine plays its part in that chorus: it knows its place, it loves it and is happy; every blade of grass grows and is happy! Everything has its path, and everything knows its path; it departs with a song and it comes back with a song; only he knows nothing, understands nothing, neither men nor sounds, a stranger to everything and an outcast.

(Dostoyevsky, *The Idiot*)

*   *   *

When first I lived alone in the world my mentors were gay boys in the Village who thought life meant going into the streets, cruising someone and bringing him home for sex, sometimes several times in one day or night. I didn't live it, but I considered it might be intriguing.

Al was a short, pleasant-looking fellow in his early twenties with blue eyes and brown hair that he wore flattened down and parted on one side. He was a pal of Bill's, or, rather, hung around with Bill and Bill's friends. When you went cruising, you had to know if the apartment was going to be empty or not, so you offered your place if the other guy didn't have one. Al knew he could go to

Bill's if Steve, his own lover, who worked odd hours as a hospital orderly, wasn't at work, because Bill was always at work. He could mention it to Bill later. A lot of people had keys to Bill's apartment.

Early one morning I happened to run into Al on the corner, and as we walked down Sixth Avenue, I looked at the men we passed, trying to see through Al's eyes the sexual fuselage he was seeking in a guy. For a quick encounter. A dark stocky fellow crossed our path, but just as I saw his eyes meet Al's, I had to run for the bus. When I saw Al again in a week's time, I couldn't resist asking if he had gone home with the fellow. After thinking back for a moment or two, he replied that he had. Had it been good I asked, wanting to know what they had done, how they had done it—in which positions—and who had done what to whom? But because he didn't offer to tell me, I didn't allow myself to ask.

*   *   *

At last I was going to find out what was meant by life. The real thing. The guides in the process of my initiation were numerous gay boys I met and befriended. Boys who thought fucking was the same as breathing and whose connection to a stranger was everything and anything.

They cared for little but sexual conquest. By day they worked at meaningless jobs, their real lives began and flourished at night. Behind the bushes in the park, in bars, in men's rooms. On the street. It was a trick you could always perform, a gift given and a gift kept. Getting lost in someone else's ecstasy meant your own could take root. At the same time that it was all those things, it was exactly the opposite. I thirsted for a knowledge about these ways of being in the world that would imprint itself on me.

Hinton was someone I saw every day; we worked in the same building. We had lunch. Patrician looks, graceful hands, soft southern burred speech. Fair curly hair. Cruising Central Park at night. He told his adventures. How at home in Virginia as a young man he had taken a guy into his bed and given the guy a jar of cold cream to rub on Hinton's cock, as he blew the guy, and how great it had felt. While I blew'm was what he said in his low melodious voice. I sat opposite him in the cafeteria. How he had sat on a man's lap on a park bench, being fucked in the ass, then pulling out of the guy at the end so he could kneel down and take the guy's load in his mouth. As much as he wanted to talk, I wanted to listen, I couldn't listen enough. How a boy in the next department was cruising him and that he was interested and one day, behind the stacks in the library, he had briefly felt the guy's cock and it was a good size. How his three-year-old nephew's cock was not quite the size of his pinky, and he held up his pinky to show me. I existed to listen to Hinton's stories; he existed to tell them to me. How he met an older man in the park who had lost his young lover and wanted Hinton to spend the night with him so they could sleep like spoons and the old guy could keep Hinton's cock between his legs as they slept because he had slept that way with his lover for seventeen years. How he cruised the men's room at Radio City Music Hall on his lunch hour and rimmed a guy before he blew him. How a friend of his, Fran Murphy and his lover, Marty, always took Fran's mother with them when they went on trips, and how much respect Marty always showed for Fran's mother. How Marty had to have a lover in addition to Fran because Fran's cock, too short to get past Marty's sphincter muscle during intercourse, caused him too much pain, but that they were a couple anyway and had been for years. The security guard of the building where we worked, Patrick O'Gallagher, was a courteous old gentleman who greeted me with a smile whenever he saw me. Hinton told me they chatted sometimes and that O'Gallagher asked him if it got hard when he saw me or when Hinton and I were deep in conversation together on our coffee breaks. Hinton said that he told him it did, and that O'Gallagher nodded understanding-ly and smiled at him.

I had met Kate. For the first time in my life, I was able to feel close to someone. Twinned. There was something essential between Kate and me that didn't exist with anyone else in the world. Nor, I thought, for her.

I loved. Was loved. So it seemed. My real life had truly begun.

*   *   *

But had not Kate come in one evening looking sweaty and overworked, her face flushed, saying she had spent the day—as she sometimes did—reading philosophy texts in Central Park where, she said, it was her custom to perform blow jobs on some of the elderly men who came to sit on the benches in the sun. Just imagine, she was lighting a cigarette as she spoke, some of these men haven't had sex for years, and probably weren't expecting to, ever again. What a good thing I've done for them. Kate took a puff on her cigarette. A good deed, really, she blew out smoke. Don't touch me Doris said as Kate leaned towards her for a kiss. I don't want you to touch me. Kate looked at her. What's wrong? she asked, I was doing them a favor. It was such a hot day.

Get away from me was all Doris could force out, her eyes hooded.

Kate drew close to her again looking puzzled. What's wrong, why are you acting so strange. Why won't you kiss me?

Doris said, go home and take a bath.

Kate looked at her. If I do that, will you kiss me? Why can't you just kiss me now?

I just can't. I don't want you to touch me.

Don't make such a big thing out of nothing. I was doing those poor old men a favor. None of them could ever get it up on their own anymore, you can be sure of that. I took pity on them. Surely you don't mind. Do you?

Doris felt herself recoil from this total stranger who was Kate. Take a bath. Scrub yourself with soap and hot water before you come near me, she said through her teeth.

All right, all right, said Kate. I'll come back tomorrow after work.

Doris felt Kate draw close to her again. She could smell the dampness of Kate's sweat and see the flushed skin of her cheek and neck. Just get out, she could barely utter the words.

After Kate left, Doris thought about her horror. She felt sickened by Kate's betrayal, but it was the acting out of her fantasy, Doris knew, that couldn't be borne. Kate's fantasy was do-able, was perfectly real and that was what Doris didn't want to know. Kate's ability to act it out, something she, Doris, couldn't do, didn't want to do. To act it out might mean piercing reality in such a way that reality might never again come back to her. That was her fear. Kate was dangerous; to be near her was dangerous. You couldn't know what she might do.

Less than two months later, Kate returned from a job interview and let slip that she and her interviewer had had sex. She had sucked him off right after the interview she said. An older man with a beard. Bald. It was a vaguely clerical job—running the office or being a cashier, something that was far below the level of Kate's abilities. Doris understood Kate's despair at having to take such a job, how much it tore away at her image of herself as a philosopher and metaphysician. Nevertheless, a hundred questions flooded Doris's mind; she asked none of them. In a choked voice she demanded why, why did you do it, knowing the fruitlessness of her question. He wanted me to, Kate answered.

He looked at me in a certain way.

She told Kate she wanted her to leave.

Kate left for her mother's saying she would be back in three days. Doris did not know why she accepted this. Don't come back until Thursday, she said.

Kate's appetite for betrayal was far beyond Doris's powers. She did not know what to do about it except to feel trapped by Kate's power over her, feel unable to protect herself or move out from underneath it.

It did not occur to her that Kate might change, nor did she

think she could change so that she would not care what Kate did. She could not leave Kate.

*   *   *

Kate lived with me most of the week in my tiny apartment, a fifth-floor walkup in the Village. Once a week she went home to change clothes. Otherwise she ate and slept with me, my every move her business. She was my jail, I her prisoner. If I went to the public library six blocks away to return my books, she'd check the time I left, the time I returned, and want to know the details if it took five minutes longer than she expected. Had I lingered to talk with someone there or on the way back? For a year the flesh of my neck was scarlet with hickeys made deliberately by her so that everyone could see them as marks of her possession of me.

One of the fellows who worked in another department came up to me one day to ask who had done that to my neck, it was a disgrace. My boyfriend, I quickly answered. Don't they hurt, he inquired, shaking his head in disbelief when I said they did not. I thought that everyone who saw Kate and me together could tell we were lovers and some of the time I was proud of being so passionately desired, some of the time I did not know what I felt. Kate was of such beauty people in the street would sometimes stop in their tracks to stare at her. Sometimes they followed her. One day on the IRT subway a woman stared at her for forty-five minutes from the heart of Brooklyn to the heart of Manhattan. When Kate got off at her stop, the woman leaped up, got off, and asked Kate to go home with her. When Kate refused—she always read a book on the train with great concentration but always knew when she was being stared at even as she pretended not to know—the woman continued to follow her, asking for her address and phone number. But Kate said she was on her way to work so she did not go with the woman.

Another time, a woman approached Kate at the Museum and invited her to her apartment for a drink. After their arrival at the apartment, the woman left the room for a few minutes and reappeared totally nude as Kate sat in the living room waiting for her to return with the drinks.

Kate smiled at her recollection and shook her head. People just don't realize how shy I am, she said. I'm terribly shy. I just had to leave when she came out like that without any clothes on.

Within five years of Kate's dogging my every move, my desire to escape from her was as great as my fear of her leaving me. She would refuse to speak if she were angry about any infractions—large or small—that I committed. It was by instinct that she understood and played upon my weaknesses. She would close herself in silence; she would sleep for days. Not a word to say, nothing to give, her refusal to touch me, to acknowledge my existence drove me to desperation. Sometimes as she lay disdainfully asleep I thought of grabbing a kitchen knife and cutting her throat so as to be free of her. More than once I stood and glared with hatred at her small sleeping form, the bread knife—a dull thing at its best—gripped tight in my hands for a long time before I finally put it down. The only way I could get away from Kate, I thought, would be to throw myself from the roof, but I didn't know how to find my way upwards; the roof seemed eons away.

I was trapped, a weakling. But at the same time I had the power to attract a woman named Lois, an amiable blonde Amazon with whom I quickly fell into an affair. Suddenly it was easy to lie to Kate. Early Saturday mornings I took the subway uptown for the Columbia University Library to do the weekly research for the graduate courses that were required for my job. My work went like the wind; I could finish in two hours what it took the rest of my class eight to accomplish. There was enough time left to take the train to Lois's apartment in the Village—across town from where Kate and I lived—where Lois and I spent every Saturday afternoon in bed. For the pleasure of lying in Lois's arms, her lightness, her laughter, her agreeableness, versus Kate's haughty brilliance, her darkness and passiveness, it seems to me I could have done almost anything.

If Stilitano were to add to his power over me by giving me any wild hope, he would reduce me to slavery. I already found myself floundering in a deep, sad element. And what were Stilitano's flurries holding in store for me? I said to him, "You know, I still have a soft spot for you, and I'd like to make love to you."

Without looking at me, he answered smilingly, "We'll see about it."

After a brief silence he said, "What do you feel like doing?"

"With you, everything!"

"We'll see."

He didn't budge. No movement bore him toward me, though my whole being wanted to be swallowed up within him, though I wanted to give my body the suppleness of osier so as to twine around him, though I wanted to warp, to bend over him. The city was exasperating. The smell of the port and its excitement inflamed me.

(Genet, *The Thief's Journal*)

I did not cease during this time to make love with Kate. And within a few months of beginning the affair with Lois, I found myself toying with the idea of starting another affair with a woman named Sylvia, a writer who worked in another department who presented herself to me.

Between my assignations with Lois, and sleeping with Kate, I thought of nothing but lovemaking. The more sexual I became, the more I wanted sex. Lois had been living with her lover for six years; sex had been absent from their lives for almost as long. She hadn't realized, she said, with her ready smile, how much she missed feeling erotic until I'd catapulted myself into the midst of her life two months earlier.

Sylvia had had a woman lover, a sort of half-hearted affair, but she sometimes thought about the possibility of others.

Kate had had many more lovers than I, but I did not allow myself to worry about disease or germs; after all, she was my lover. Sex was the anodyne, a delicious game one could play, the more of it the better. I envied the boys their ruttishness, their easy promiscuity, something I could never match except in fantasy. I wanted to be depraved; it was my body's and soul's path towards corruption. I steeped myself in Genet's books: *The Thief's Journal, Our Lady of the Flowers* and followed in my own way his exquisite masturbatory imagination, an erotic sensibility which felt familiar, spread out in me and became, with few changes, mine as far as I could go with it. It required little work for me to feel how low I'd sunk—a depth I wanted and wanted to explore. To find pleasure in my sense of degradation, to soak myself in sex with three women, to lie to each of them. To keep doing it with the arrogance of a woman of twenty-six who imagines she has no one to answer to but herself. What was it I was trying to prove?

When might I finally leap into the heart of the image, be myself the light which carries it to your eyes? When might I be in the heart of poetry?

I run the risk of going astray by confounding saintliness with solitude. But am I not, by this sentence, running the risk of restoring to saintliness the Christian meaning which I want to remove from it?

The quest for transparency may be vain. If attained, it would be repose. Ceasing to be "I," ceasing to be "you," the subsisting smile is a uniform smile cast upon all things.

(Genet, *The Thief's Journal*)

I practiced the lessons my friends taught me.

When I invited Sylvia home with me after having dinner with her on one of the week nights Kate was away at her new teaching job, we ended up in the only bed in the apartment, the one I slept in with Kate.

Sylvia was the opposite of Lois; dark and Latin, a little taller than me, but lean with big bones. She was amiable and not particularly sensual, but she wanted to please. Sylvia was the obliging person I seemed to require to balance Kate's dour energy. I hungered for Sylvia the way Lois wanted me, ferociously. No, that isn't true. Lois was a teddy bear, laughing and snuggling, waiting to be pushed or pulled into her next move, the ferociousness was mine. But Lois gave something back.

With Kate, lovemaking was ritual, always the same. It soothed us; she would become filled with my energy, a life infusion she required of me. She took the sonar signals I sent from the heart—the kind of exploratory signals porpoises send—but she did not return them or complete the circle, she kept them. She hoarded them. At the time, I knew nothing, understood nothing.

I moved as if in a dream.

To go from one bed to another, from one person to another wasn't the same as picking up strangers, but it served; for me it had the same effect. I reveled in it. I was like them, I thought, free. Free to be depraved.

Saying of them "They're treacherous" softened my heart. Still softens me at times. They are the only ones I believe capable of all kinds of boldness. Their sinuousness and the multiplicity of their moral lines form an interlacing which I call adventure. They depart from your rules. They are not faithful. After all, they have a blemish, a wound, comparable to the bunch of grapes in Stilitano's underpants. In short, the greater my guilt in your eyes, the more whole, the more totally assumed, the greater will be my freedom. The more perfect my solitude and uniqueness. By my guilt I further gained the right to intelligence. Too many people think, I said to myself, who don't have the right to. They have not paid for it by the kind of undertaking which makes thinking indispensable to your salvation.

This pursuit of traitors and treason was only one of the forms of eroticism. It is rare—it is almost unknown—for a boy to offer me the heady joy that can only be offered me by the interlacings of a life in which I would be involved with him. A body stretched out between my sheets, fondled in a street or at night in the woods, or on a beach, affords me half a pleasure: I dare not see myself loving it, for I have known too many situations in which my person, whose importance lay in its grace, was the factor of charm of the moment. I shall never find them again. Thus do I realize that I have sought only situations charged with erotic intentions. That was what, among other things, guided my life. I am aware that there exist adventures whose heroes and details are erotic. Those are the ones I have wanted to live.

(Genet, *The Thief's Journal*)

Broken

Alison had returned from Southeast Asia six months before, a trip she had taken with her husband, to see how the people lived who live close to nature, eat sticky rice three times a day, learn from nature how to live like, how to be, nature. Not, as we Americans and Europeans and as she had been taught to "align ourselves with nature," for the Southeast Asians were already aligned, already non-separated, had never been disconnected, had always been part of, had always been, nature.

In an article Alison wrote that was published in a macrobiotic magazine, to show her appreciation, to acknowledge her debt, to indicate that she understood the way of no separation, she pointed out that in her cooking classes she always advocated, made a point of explaining, telling her students not to use the same three or four vegetables every day; they must vary them, must change them, not three or four but seven or eight at least. Variety was so important, the body would not benefit without it.

The body required change or it grew tired, bored, estranged. Eating the same foods all the time made the body become tight. It needed difference. After a while Alison saw that the Nepalese people among whom she lived for six months with Rupert, her husband, were eating the same three or four vegetables every day. They ate what they grew, what grew under their feet, what their neighbors grew, and it was the same dish always, cooked maybe a little differently, maybe the same, a bit higher flame sometimes or more seasoning. But, here they were, the people of no separation, eating and drinking always the same food, what they grew, just the opposite of what she had been taught and what she believed and was teaching and had taught all of her cooking students: variety.

Now that she had returned from her eye-opening trip to Nepal, she was possessed by strange body heat and odd fevers at all hours of the day and night. She did not understand the reason.

123

Odd high fevers that so far did not respond to the Oriental folk remedies she had been taught to use. A sickness she could neither explain nor get rid of. So far it had lasted for months, almost a year. Her body's interior seemed on fire; nothing could cool her.

In the midst of her sickness, she came to New York from Los Angeles to lecture about traditional healing foods and lifestyles on a day when she was feeling a little better than usual. Still, her face was flushed.

I made an appointment to see her after the lecture. A private session.

I wanted to know what she thought might be the best course of treatment for the lump in my breast and the general malaise I had been feeling off and on for years. I explained this over the phone. We had met once six years earlier but I could not recall her face.

I walked into the room. She sat opposite me and leaned to one side in her chair. She was about thirty-five, red-faced with blue eyes, and brown hair that reached to her shoulders. Eyes fixed on my face, she uttered her first words.

"So tell me about the stuff with your mother."

"My mother? It was my father." I said it low, suddenly mistrustful of her and whatever she was going to say. Her speech seemed to tumble from deep inside herself. She projected her words like a volcano spits flame.

"Not enough of an active and lively circulation." She flicked her eyes over me, then looked into my eyes. "Too middle of the road. You need more strong circulation to give you polarity. A stronger surge inside and throughout your body to get things moving."

She paused, looking me over.

"Your underlying emotional condition is oppressed from within."

She nodded her head slightly to herself. As if she were satisfied with this pronouncement

I was riveted to my chair. I wanted to hide. This was going to be worse than I thought.

"You don't fully inhabit your space on the earth. *Every single day you need a thousand depth-charged hugs.*"

For what? I almost broke in. *For what do I need them?*

I didn't dare speak.

"You have emotional emptiness. Deep emotional emptiness. You've been deeply neglected by someone you really miss."

Who was it, I wanted to interrupt her. *Was it Mama? Or Sheila? My lovers? Was it one of them or all of them?*

"You went without that kind of nourishment all your life. Didn't get the deep strokes you needed. And you want someone to just know that and give it to you. But you don't, you can't ask for it."

I was choked up with wanting to stop her, but I couldn't open my mouth.

"No," she went on, looking just past me towards the center of the room, "you can't ask for it, but you must get the attention you need in healthy ways."

"Healthy ways." I repeated the words to myself with a certain amount of scorn at the phrase.

Those words. The last resort of those who seek to apprehend the world through the mind. Can't understand the world by any other means. Deem the senses inaccurate.

Just what is your definition of health? I wanted to demand. *Is it you? Are you the arbiter, the perfect model of health?*

I said nothing.

She went on. "In too many areas you have servant energy."

"But servants are often leaders," I interrupted her. "What about Leo the servant in Herman Hesse's *Journey to the East?*

"That's a different kind of servant. Yours is the other kind. The wrong kind. The servant energy, not the servant.

"You aren't being loved and nourished so you can come to life."

I was silent. I knew what my choices had been.

They had been wrong.

What did she see when she looked at me? It was true I had been a servant, but my servant energy had seemed ecstatic and powerful to me. It was my fire, the purest kind of energy. I experienced pleasure in serving though it was true, I'd often felt used. Not only had I allowed it, I had gotten something from it.

I'd never said no.

By now I knew that not a soul I had chosen had had it in them to give me what I wanted; it was a charge I'd have to create for myself. Nobody outside of me was going to give it to me.

Lois had served me. I had desired her sexual love of me and I'd celebrated it. But I hadn't loved her, wasn't in emotional thrall to her. To me her mind and emotions seemed hopelessly childish even as I'd admired and loved her body and the sexual power over me she didn't begin to guess she had. Desired her physical domination of me, willingly gave her my body even as I knew I could not leave Kate to whom I was in emotional thrall; I was Kate's prisoner, her servant, because Kate held my emotional strings, Lois did not. Maybe I had to be in thrall or I couldn't really be served. But, didn't being in thrall mean I was the servant? If only, I thought, Lois had the emotional wits to hold me, I'd be hers. Kate had enough wits to hold me but didn't really have me, couldn't make me feel what Lois could. I hated Kate as much as I loved her. Maybe that was love.

My head swam.

"You have major love and forgiveness issues," Alison's voice bit the air. "And you're leaking energy from the left side of your body."

Leaking energy out of my heart side? I thought. My left side contained the pent-up liver qi stagnation, my too-many-years-too-much-stress. Hongwei Zhu, my acupuncturist, had explained this to me many times.

My shen. My spirit which is housed in the heart.

Wounded. Leaking.

Alison sat down and looked earnest. "Don't give your spirit away to the early trauma with your father," she said sternly. "You cannot have your father be in charge of your life. You have to work on this to get yourself to a place where there's no emotional charge there for you any more.

"I want you to have a lot of compassion for the little girl who was you. Say to her, 'I'm sorry I couldn't take care of you.'"

I couldn't answer her.

"Do you have a picture of yourself as a little girl?"

I nodded, just barely. In spite of myself.

"You must take care of the child you were who couldn't protect herself. You must be healed of the bad stuff happening again, your vulnerability.

"Your first step is to do the healing work to the little girl. Then to be compassionate towards your father and his sickness. You must embrace and become one with all your demons."

She rattled it off like a lesson she had memorized.

"This is your homework. You have a huge lesson in mistrust ahead of you until you graduate from the position of victimization you've put yourself into. You've got to be able to say, 'I can love and embrace all my abusers.'"

No, no, no, I said silently.

"Otherwise, you give your heart away. You gave it away.

"Fear and mistrust have made your kidneys dry. Fear and resentment is contraction. Forgiveness is divine. You've got to be able to say and feel, 'Heal this poor broken person who is me and my dad.'"

Was there no end to this? *No,* I swore silently. *I am not broken.*

"Have compassion for him. Say thank you, father. But remember," she sped through this part so rapidly that I could barely take it in, "if you forgive your abuser without compassion for yourself, you shut yourself out of your own heart."

No, I repeated to myself, *I am not broken.*

She looked at me one last time.

"Ask for guidance," she said.

I could barely stand up.

I was emptied.

Unsteady on my feet.

Before walking out of the room, I stepped gingerly towards her for the goodbye hug she'd insist on. Her body was inert, a taut, unknowable container.

Her version of me was dead wrong. Twisted. True only a small portion of the time. The chemistry of her presence and my presence together stripped me of any power I had and brought out the worst in me. If someone less judgemental would see me differently I would expand in that image of myself. At the moment it was my luck to feel kayoed, against the wall, by a woman whose opinion I knew now I didn't want, but had gone out of my way to get.

To some people I was a child, sunny and playful, a vision of myself I genuinely preferred. To others I was oppressed hopelessly from within. I needed to avoid thinking about what she had said, but it was there, listing about in the sea of my feelings, a loosely tied boat.

What was true? I wanted to invoke the descriptions other people had offered me of myself to compare them with Alison's. See where the balance lay.

The truth was always changing because it depended on the waxing and waning energies of the viewer. The way energy could move from one person into another reminded me of the end of Hesse's *Journey to the East*, the way energy poured into one image from the other.

Only a few months before, Alison's teacher had told me I was gentle on the outside and strong on the inside. His description of me had been the opposite of Alison's. Could I have changed so much in so short a time?

Sensitive heart and emotions, he had said, *your energy is softer and less sharp than that of most people. You are independent yet you are insecure at the same time; dependent and independent, both.*

The month in which you were born, December, is the coldest and darkest month. It has the shortest days and it is opposite June, which is the most yang month, December is the most yin month with its cold and water. You have strong energy inside you from birth. Since you were born in December, you were conceived in March; there are always three months of the year that we lack in our experience before birth, three months are the pieces we lack. They are what we long for, what we crave. What we crave turns out to be our physical and mental condition, different from our constitution which is what we inherit from our ancestors. What we are born with.

He went on: *Reading your face according to Oriental diagnosis, your face shows darkness on the right side. The right side is earth's force, the force which governs dreams, aspirations, wishes and the fulfillment of wishes. And while your right side shows that you are going towards a clear vision, it shows that you haven't yet arrived there.*

Your left side, which represents the force of heaven's influence in your life, is the practical, material side and it shows your determination to see things through. Your heaven's force is lighter, brighter than your earth's force.

In your face, dark layers are peeling away from the past and you are moving towards brightness but you are not there.

You need to make everything move within yourself. Things from the past must be shaken up. You need some extremes to throw the excess from your past back into circulation;

You are much stronger than you appear.

Most people won't understand this about you.

Doris goes to see Chunyan Teng, an acupuncturist in New York recommended to her by one of her classmates, for a consultation about the lump in her breast and her general condition.

She waits for the answers and wonders how they will compare with what Hongwei Zhu, the other acupuncturist, has told her about herself.

"You keep everything inside," Dr. Teng announces in a high voice. She speaks rapidly and without Western expressiveness. "You are emotionally withdrawn. Must open chest, make energy come out. Use local acupuncture points 3-4, Ren 17, Pericardium 6, Stomach 36, Spleen 4. Those points must be used to open chest.

"Never see loud, extrovert person come in with problem like

yours. Loud extrovert person angry, blow off steam; but you, you keep all inside. Creates liver blood stagnation, liver qi stagnation; difficult for you generate blood."

"Emotionally withdrawn? Are you saying I am emotionally withdrawn?" Doris wants to know.

"Ah no," Chunyan corrects herself. "Emotionally suppressed. Keep everything inside."

Doris doesn't want to accept the truth or falseness of this statement, but hearing it makes her uneasy.

Alison's teacher tells her about her hands.

"The square under the index finger is the mark of the teacher. And the grid that shows underneath your little finger is the sign of the healer. You have both," he says. He pauses and looks at the base of both of her index fingers. *"The Ring of Solomon,"* he announces; *"you have the Ring of Solomon on the index fingers of both hands!"*

"The Ring of Solomon?"

"Wisdom. Intuition." He held her hands open and pointed out the swirl, the flesh that was curved underneath the skin. *"The kind you get from going through a lot. Experience. But also,"* he paused and looked at her face, *"it comes from your ancestors, maybe that's where you got some of it. But to have it on both fingers!*

"Your heartline is deep and strong but it has a gentle curve which means that you can relate to different kinds of people and have an understanding of different sides—yourself and people totally different from yourself.

"A person like you has vision, the vision to do what they want; one can rely on them; they have integrity."

On her first visit to Hongwei Zhu, Doris mentions that she is studying Chinese Herbology.

Hongwei Zhu says to her, "You study herbs? Really? Where?" Hongwei wants to know immediately.

"In New York."

"But you are a teacher, no?"

"I am a teacher, yes."

"Then you study herbs as hobby," Hongwei flatly concludes, as if she knows exactly that that is the case.

"No," Doris says, "not a hobby."

"You want practice as an herbalist? You want see patients?"

"No," Doris says, "not exactly."

Hongwei waits.

"I want to learn. I have a thirst for knowledge."

Hongwei looks at her and shakes her head. "It is hobby," she says as if it is a new American word she has just learned.

"Hongwei, I study Chinese herbology so I can understand some things about Chinese Medicine. I want you to treat the root of the problems I have, not the branch or the leaf.

"Yes, yes, I understand." Hongwei is smiling but she doesn't look directly at Doris. "All right. I treat like you want. I understand. I respect your wish." She makes a slight bow. "You are right."

No matter how much Hongwei says out loud that she agrees with Doris's opinions, she will not tell Doris what she is doing, nor the exact nature of her treatment plan. Grudgingly, she will sometimes offer, "This help your liver and spleen, help reduce your stress. Your stress level very high. Must lower."

Alison's teacher tells her the following: *"Nature has two characteristics: complete predictable order, where the sun rises and the sun sets, and complete unpredictability—we can never tell what will happen at any day or hour. If you want to be free, be like Nature. That opens your life to many possibilities. Want to know balance? Make your life like Nature, a combination of orderliness and inconsistency."*

*   *   *

China was originally an agricultural society, so the Chinese saw and described the whole world in relation to the seasons. Which can be seen in terms of one person and the passage of one day in the life of the person, as if it is their whole life.

According to Chinese Medicine, disease is an invitation to

change. Wind brings about change. Wind is the cause of hundreds of diseases. Wind travels upwards and lifts up. Wind tells us we can't stay in one place. Animals under stress move around, pace, try to find ease.

Dampness is characterized by something that begins to slow down, that lingers around, like fog. People who are damp slow down more. Like fog. You are in a fog.

Thoughts not clear.

Not the straight path of a wood person.

A wood person is clear about pushing a chair straight across the floor to its destination going neither to the left nor to the right. A damp person will push the chair every which way along an uneven path. As if her destination is unclear, possibly unknown.

Coaxing the Pudding

She heard R. speak the words, "and I coaxed the pudding." Seated at the table, they were finishing the dinner they had cooked and gazing at the fat white candle R. had lit between them.

"You're good at that," Doris said. "You should concentrate on doing whatever you're good at."

There was a long silence, their eyes meeting and R.'s clouding over, the pure blue color deepening with her look of understanding of the underneath of "coaxing the pudding." Her eyes met Doris's and they sat, eyes locked, without uttering a word.

Hearing the words "I coaxed the pudding" made Doris feel coaxed. At last. God, how she wanted to be coaxed.

She broke into a sweat which R. knew nothing about.

Was her good karma going to come due at last? Was she going to get something she really wanted? Would it truly happen? Was she going to be coaxed, cosseted, held and petted? *Really* held? If only she could keep her hands quiet, refrain from moving them, maybe it would happen. Caressed the way she wanted to be. If she could only do the right thing, allow herself to receive without thinking she had to return every caress two or threefold, maybe it would happen. If it could happen, it might change her, the lump in her breast would melt, go away, she would be found.

She heard the word "coax" and had been filled immediately with desire and a kind of emotion she had never before known. She knew R. had the power to coax pleasure from her—or was it something she just imagined and projected onto R.? To rain down pleasure with a few caresses, to coax from her the pleasure that was waiting to be coaxed. R. could do it, it was what Doris had been waiting for.

At the sound of R.'s words she became the pudding coaxed into fullness, ripeness, consistency, creaminess. She believed that R., who did not appear overly powerful on the surface, had the power nevertheless to coax from her the beauty of an orgasm by just staying with her, being there with her, the thing Doris most needed and somehow never got because she was always giving, always being there for someone else. Giving the other what *she* wanted. For her to come, she needed to know she would not be abandoned, she would be stayed with until the end. No matter what, the what being an unclear entity.

She knew also that R. might not be that way at all, that it could be projection, that the R. who existed was in actuality entirely different from her dream of R. and might never, couldn't ever give her what it was that she most wanted.

Doris had gone from being a lover who was proud of her sexual prowess to being a long time unloved. It was her sexual karma, she guessed, the punishment for her pride, her arrogance; she could make anyone come, something she discovered mainly by accident; that was how it started for her, just by knowing how to be there for someone. An accident of birth, or maybe her true nature, she did not know. Now she could not come; it had been taken from her.

The longing was for her an ancient longing, her lack a central cause of the yin fire, the condition of consciously suppressed longing, an emotion whose existence created the internal conflagration from which she suffered.

Maybe it is possible my body will be reborn in the presence of the one who waits for me. Who doesn't stop in the middle, or leave off and say she's too tired to continue once I have satisfied her, waited for her, been there for her, let her know she could take her time. "Take your time," Doris had often murmured to her lovers. "I am not in a hurry." They were the words everyone wanted to hear, but that Doris had never heard anyone say, to let her know they were there, would be there, no matter what.

The words "just be there" were a mantra she hadn't uttered to anyone. Hadn't dared.

In the years she had spent satisfying the sexual needs of her lovers with her servant energy, she had always wanted to say the words "just be there" to someone just as *she* had been there.

She had never been able to utter them in the face of her feeling that she, with her own needs, was just too much trouble, wasn't worth it, didn't deserve from her lovers what she herself gave. Wasn't worth it.

To have uttered the words aloud would have meant asking for something she knew they could not give. Blood from a stone. Milk from a mother whose breasts were dry. Succor for a beggar asking for food. Hopeless to ask for something you doubted could be given.

She did not ask.

She could depend on herself to give to others and her lovers could always depend on her. When she twisted the tendon of her right elbow by carrying something the wrong way, hefting a gallon jug of water, and was told by the doctor that the injury would take at least six weeks to heal, she trained her left hand and arm for lovemaking and worked to make it perfect for her lover Sasha so that there would be no interruption in the pattern of their lovemaking. Not even a day. So that Sasha would not fail to feel just as satisfied with her left as she had with her right. It worked, it seemed to be perfect, although being naturally very right-handed it was difficult for Doris, a difficulty she brushed away. She made it clear that her discomfort did not matter to her, so it did not matter to her lover.

She grew used to not being able to depend on anyone to be there; she gave up the desire to ask any of her lovers to *just be there,* even Sasha; she felt it was hopeless. To her lovers it must have seemed that she was always ready for them if they made the merest gesture of desire.

She guessed they thought that she liked to give more than she liked to receive. They did not seem to know or care that she was left wanting. She almost always said that it did not matter, it was O.K., although she did not say it in a terribly convincing way even if they questioned her, which was not often. She did not want to be burdensome; she assumed she would never get what she wanted anyway.

She noticed that the more sex women were given, the more love, the less patient or desirous they were of returning it. On the contrary, they wanted to receive more, whereas the less she got, the more she had to make do with it, pretend it was enough. She had often said, "Later, you'll take care of me later. You should rest for a while now." She turned her desire to be loved, desired, cosseted, petted, into making love to her lovers: cosseting, petting them into feeling loved, bathed in love. If "later" sometimes came for her, the chemistry was wrong; it seemed flat; they were performing a duty; it was not from desire—which made her uncomfortable and tense.

She thought of this "later" often; but she hid her disappointment and took pride in bestowing on her lovers the instinctive and learned talents of her body until her lovers were sated. It was the lump in her breast that received her disappointment. Her yin fire. And it grew.

Body

Doris discovered how to take the floor in a class at the New Dance Group Studio in Manhattan.

One day her teacher told each person in the class to walk across the floor as if she owned it. Hold the stage with your presence. Who you are. On the diagonal, from one end of the studio to the other.

She could not do it.

It was after she broke both middle toes of her left foot against the rock jetty of a beach in South Carolina that she was able to take the floor with a modicum of authority. Such purpose had inflamed her stride across the sand, she had not noticed the hardness of the jetty until it struck her. Then it was the pain she noticed. Her real presence was to arrive much later.

One night when I was fifteen, I stayed late at school to play the "Christe Eleison" of the Bach B Minor Mass over and over until the library closed at six.

It was the dead of winter. Patches of ice, visible and invisible, mirrored the cloudy sky and the streetlights on every gutter and sidewalk of the city. It was dark when I boarded the subway. I rocked back and forth in the dim light of the coach as if in a dream, then scrambled my way upstairs to wait for the bus that would take me the next part of the trip.

It was the last leg. Six deserted streets lay before me.

I struggled for a comfortable angle at which to grasp my satchel, which was loaded with schoolbooks. I walked quickly down the first hill, the only sound the click of my shoes on the ice. It came to me suddenly that I was the one who was destined to stay and listen to the "Christe Eleison" of the B Minor Mass until the library closed, while everyone else in the world safely warmed themselves at the table of all the kitchens and homes that ever existed.

There were only a few bars of the music that moved me to

137

ecstasy, but I needed to prolong those moments more than I needed food or companionship.

I played them over and over.

It seemed to me that it was my destiny to make my way without the comfort of being ensconced in the embrace of a loving family. Something about the sound of the double bass and the violoncello, against which the duet of soprano and mezzo-soprano harmonized the line of the melody, created a feeling of utter solitude and unspeakable longing in me. As clearly as I could see the warmth and brightness of everyone else's situation, I needed to hold the feeling of the music, nourish it and make it glow in the darkness of my belly. It was the purity of my aloneness. My life's blood. Recognizing my position in life, and lost thus for the moment, I slid and fell with all my might on the ice. A moan of pain escaped my lips, an intake of breath that took a full two minutes to be exhaled. I got to my feet laboriously. My shaking hands took hold of my satchel and I continued walking as best I could.

I told no one what had occurred. I do not know why I did not utter a word when I arrived home about what had happened to me. Surely someone would have listened, though I could barely speak from agony.

From that day, I suffered back pain without surcease; the wound was mine to be borne.

It was after the fall, the pain of the wound, made deeper without solace, that, fully alive in my body, I was able to walk across the floor and hold the stage with my presence, albeit wounded.

*   *   *

The doctor wrote and asked me to return his call. We want to treat you because your sister was a psychotic patient from a dysfunctional family whom we treated at the Institute during her adolescence. As her younger sister, you should have been treated at the same time. Although it is fifteen years later, we would like to offer to you a full course of psychotherapy. Will you accept this gift from us, an attempt on our part to straighten out our books—so to speak? A follow-up.

I said that I would.

Would I prefer a woman therapist or a man?

I told them I would prefer a woman.

I went to see Dr. Hannah Beraikh once a week at her light-filled, spacious apartment that overlooked the green fastness of Central Park. I was always twenty minutes to a half hour late. I did not know why I could not stop being late.

I paid her $17.00 a visit which was a lot of money for me; my earnings were $148.00 a month working at the Main Edifice of the New York Public Library Research Collection, couchant lions in front, as a page in the stacks running for books that were requested by the library patrons seven flights above me. They scrawled out on small request forms the authors, titles and call numbers they wanted, which were then sealed in small metal boxes and dispatched to the proper stack via mechanical chute, which made a loud gasp as it was suctioned rapidly into the tunnel. On their arrival they were grabbed out of the boxes, read by us, the pages, and run for at top speed down the gleaming marble floors. We brought the books back, set them in baskets, request slips inserted inside the books, and sent them upwards on a dumbwaiter. Without catching our breaths.

Winter or summer, whenever I had a moment during the day, I looked out behind the library onto Bryant Park through the vertical stack windows that ran the length of the building. Only the windows on the highest floors looked down over the trees.

All I could think of was that I wanted to fly out the window and into the tops of the trees.

Float through the trees. That feeling.

I did not tell Dr. Beraikh about this. I told her that whenever I saw myself in the mirror on the wall of my apartment at 51 West 11th Street, I did not know who I was. The face, the eyes that gazed back at me with suspicion belonged to a stranger, a person unknown to me.

Dr. Beraikh said, "It would be better for you to not live alone; you should live with someone else during this period in your life."

In one of our first sessions, I had described in detail to Dr. Beraikh my relationship with Kate. "I think Kate is crazy," I told her. But Dr. Beraikh did not care that Kate was mad; it was more important to her that I live with a mad person than that I live alone. She did not acknowledge that she had heard me say that I thought Kate was mad.

Toward the end of my treatment with her, I asked her why she had been chosen to work with me. "I, too, had a difficult sister when I was a young girl," she said. "A very difficult sister who was adored by our parents. That is why I was chosen. It was similar, the situation." She proceeded to tell me some of the details. It did not seem similar to me.

In some people, late adolescence is accompanied by schizophrenic breaks, I had read it somewhere. The person might see something dark moving in the room beside them, out of the corner of their eye. It was more or less a normal development at that age, the text made it clear. I found in an interview with Anne Sexton the following statement, "If you want to know the truth, the leaves talk to me every June."

That was how I felt.

The leaves spoke, although I did not understand the seasons in my body, did not understand where it was that they lived inside me.

I was born in the city; it was the country that brought me to life.

*   *   *

There is no work. No money. Little food. It is cold. The first snow.

I am born in the Depression and right away my father gets a job. He can buy blankets. That is how my mother knows he's gotten a job; he comes home looking happy with blankets in his arms.

The day my mother and I come home from the hospital I am

wrapped in those blankets. The superintendent—an Irishman—asks if he can carry me over the threshhold, it is good luck to carry a newborn baby over a threshhold. My mother is fearful he will drop me, my father says it will be all right to let him, my parents are so happy at the turn of luck I have brought them on the first day of December that I am carried over the threshhold wrapped in a brand-new set of warm blankets. I am the good luck that is carried over the threshold by Mr. McGurn, the Irish superintendent, and put into the arms of my mother who places me gently into the crib that awaits me. The crib has bars to keep me from falling out, and, two years later, from crawling out under my own power, a thwarted attempt to end my separation from the rest of the world.

I am told many times that I bring good luck to my parents just by being born on the first of December. By the time I have grown old enough to understand this, I no longer believe it.

*   *   *

When I am ten and my breasts have already begun to slightly swell, I pretend that I am and always will be able to run around without a shirt: a boy, a son, one of the guys, a bare-shouldered, bare-chested, easy walking, easy loping boy who will never have to wear a shirt.

Not wearing a shirt means you are a boy. And though I'm not, in my heart of hearts I am.

Only a boy can be free to roam the streets, the empty lots in summer, and never have to think about wearing anything on his torso, he can be naked above and even below the waist if he chooses. While I am still ten, even though my breasts have begun to swell, I ignore them; I roam naked and free, free of being a girl.

In my heart of hearts I am a true tomboy's boy. In my heart of hearts that is where I remain despite growing up as a woman, having full breasts, and wearing bras and bathing suit tops, all of the things that hold a woman's breasts in place. In my heart of hearts I am a boy.

*   *   *

When I am only a few years older I begin to go to Mr. Geriber for piano lessons. I do not want the lessons but my mother thinks I will be jealous if Sheila, my sister, has them and I don't. Half-heartedly, I agree to go, in my colorless way—colorless whenever Sheila is around in all her color. Dutifully, I take the bus to the Grand Concourse for weekly lessons with Mr. Geriber, a squat, morose man who always reaches over to correct the arc of my hand as it is poised over the keyboard. He always manages to touch my breast.

At first I think it is accidental, and I pretend not to notice. He continues to do it. I notice and I do not know what to do about it. The one thing I do know is that, like my father, Mr. Geriber likes to fondle girls and pretend that while they are doing it everything is okay because they act as if they are not doing it while they are doing it.

After meeting me, Kate's friend Janet wrote a letter to Kate about how much she enjoyed meeting me. In the letter she described my breasts by calling them "Wot Tits!" With pride, Kate showed me the letter.

I was stunned. They must be nice if someone else likes them, I thought. From then on I decided I should be proud of them because everyone else seemed to admire them.

*   *   *

The World of the Left Hand.

My left hand was the hand I needed to help my right hand masturbate. I couldn't do it with just my right. No matter where I found myself, no matter where I was, desire drove me to lock myself into bathrooms, to crawl, to lie down so that anyone who might be looking through the window wouldn't be able to see what I was doing, to run the water so that someone might think I was taking a shower or a bath. The linoleum-covered floor, the mildew, the damp smells of summer camp for instance, where I worked as a junior counselor for three sex-filled years. To grip my flesh, to hold myself open with my left hand while the right hand did its work, to part my lips with the first two fingers of my left hand and rub my moist flesh with the index finger of the right, to use that single finger to coax, to urge, to slowly bring forth the fierce, radiating explosion, I love you I would sometimes gasp at the last moment to the shadow, the spectre of nothing, my demon, my unfeeling lover who fucked me without caring whether I liked it or not. My most intense pleasure was that my ability to come overpowered every other sensation.

*   *   *

N.B. The carapace of my past is strapped to my back, a shell, the shell of a tortoise. The very shell on which was first discovered the I Ching 5000 years ago, the signs of yin and yang which are everything in the world and nothing in the world.

It is not possible for me to speak about one of my selves without speaking of the others; they spin within me underneath the carapace that is strapped to my back.

Behind me in the train two Frenchmen murmur, deep in conversation with one another whose susurrus is continually interrupted by the other.

Voila says one, the culmination of a longish discourse. A beat; the other has picked up with *alors* and continues the flow.

One of my selves, the witness, pays heed to the pleasant rise and fall of the voices; another reads a story in the newspaper which has been left on the seat. A third observes through the window the pristine mudflats of a river in whose mirrored oily surface the sun, expanding, prepares to set.

The impenetrability of the person to whom I am bone-close is never more apparent to me than when I am with Lois or Sylvia or, especially, Kate. What does she think or feel? Does it have anything to do with me or with herself only? All this is impermeable to the roentgen rays of my perception, since I, too, am wrapped in my physical and emotional delusions, my feelings of

power and vulnerability, my notion that I exercise a control that is
both momentary and barely adequate.

The immediacy and quick passage of our meetings. Those lost
and heated events on which I could shed no light; a series of
problems that could not be solved

To forget them I would have to forget the seasons and learn
them over.

The *Potnia Theron,* the Mistress of the Animals, emerges from
her successive transformations. From the intense and dour Kate, to
Sasha, the hidden one; to You, the drunk of many sweetnesses,
your pointed fingernails uncut because your image of yourself for
others as a femme woman with long nails is more important to
you than the satisfactions of your lover who wanted to feel the
prodding of those soft-edged fingers, not their sharpened nails.

Driving to _____, Doris feels that everything is
lost, that her life is a succession of losses, that nothing survives of
her love for _____, nothing survives of Lake
Farfara, nothing of 51 West 11th, nothing of Causeway except the
distorted images of voluntary and voluptuous memory whose
gorgeous voices floated above the asphalt street Sunday mornings
from the windows of the First Baptist Church that was catercorner
to the Seacrest at the apex of Gurney Street, a sequence of
dislocations and adjustments where neither mystery nor beauty is
sacred, where all except her recollections have been consumed.

Tourist

I walk with you
into the white scrim

lost

yet found where my fears
are cheap and rancid
they flow fast
it's time for you to go, to get going,
get out, time to say
goodbye to the lump in your breast.

Accidents

When you fall, you don't anticipate hurting yourself, the *qi* of the body doesn't expect to be hurt. But if you plan, say, to kick a stone in your path, something hard, there's a readiness there, an anticipation; the body is in a different state.

In 2000 B.C. in China, the people carved into bones the details of their everyday lives in archaic languages (prior to the time of agriculture, during a time when they were hunters and gatherers).

The inscriptions they carved into the bones were a diary that recorded their ordinary lives day to day.

The shamans began to use the bones by inscribing on them the questions people asked, but only the questions which had a yes or no answer, the kind you would ask and answer an oracle.

Once the questions were inscribed with a knife, the shaman heated the bone until it cracked. Then the shaman interpreted the answer as yes or no, according to the place where the bone was cracked. Dragon bones were, in reality, fossilized dinosaur bones.

As China became agricultural, many farmers found bones with carved inscriptions as they were digging in the fields. They thought the inscriptions were messages from the gods, and, because dragons were so important in China, they believed the bones to be dragon bones.

They thought ingesting bones would calm the spirit, because, according to Classical Chinese herbology, bones are a substance that calms wind. Dragons travel through clouds, stir up the ocean and extinguish internal wind. Wind, the origin of illness, is also an invitation to change.

My first car accident: a yellow cab crashed into the rear of my Volkswagen. I had just slammed on my brakes to avoid smashing into a car that pulled out suddenly from a parking place before me on my right. Within moments a bystander ran over and said, "I'll be a witness for you; it was the cabbie's fault; he wasn't watching."

Another man waited nearby to proffer a warning, "Although you don't feel anything now, watch out for whiplash, it could show up tomorrow or the next day."

What was whiplash I wondered. I had never heard of it.

I had been on my way to the Academy of Music to attend a concert by Joan Sutherland, the coloratura known as "La Stupenda" to her admirers, with Kate and her lover, Susan, a woman much younger than she. Kate was paying Susan's tuition through graduate school. If I had stayed with Kate, she would have supported me. The conditions were simple: whenever she arrived home no matter what the time, I would have to be there. That was all.

I could not agree to these conditions. I knew there were others that were unspoken.

After the accident, I didn't see Kate for a long time—the four years and more that I wore a soft neck brace and took muscle relaxants to soothe the spasms in my neck and calm my insomnia.

One evening two years after the first accident, while driving home from work, I was stopped at a red light on a crowded street in rush hour when a car much larger than mine, driven by a corporate businessman, ploughed into the rear of my car.

The lawyers for the plaintiff contended that the symptoms I claimed from this accident stemmed from the accident I'd had two years earlier.

When the case was heard eight years later, the judge said that the numbness, the inability to concentrate, the spaceyness and headaches caused by the accident couldn't have interfered with my ability to think at my job because women didn't have jobs where they were paid just to think.

My lawyer told me that the judge, O'Mara by name, had a reputation for denseness, and was, further—he shook his head—biased against women. He was sorry to say it was just bad luck to have drawn Judge O'Mara for my case; there was nothing further that could be done.

In my ignorance, I accepted this.

The destination I chose for the month-long healing I wanted to accomplish after the accidents turned out to be a guest-house on

Gurney Street, The Seacrest, which was owned by Harriett O'Toole and located in Causeway, a small, comfortable beach town.

The center of Gurney Street held a triangle. Inside the triangle a monument reached toward the sky, an obelisk that commemorated World War II, or was it World War I? There were beds of red, white, and blue flowers planted around its base. Dying for one's country was celebrated on this peaceful street by a pointy-shaped sculpture made of cement, surrounded by ordinary white and red and blue flowers in neat rows. Across from this monument, neither stone nor brick nor roof tile of the stolid-appearing First Baptist Church had seen the smallest change over the course of generations.

The white, three-story Seacrest, shaded by maple trees, stood across from the triangle—which took up the greatest amount of space on the street, the memorial itself the least—its presence seeming to say, *There is nothing matters but now, the past will pass into dreams, the future, wisp.*

You, Gurney Street, your wide girth, you, my image, seed-bed of regret and desire, place where first I encountered Lou Chatelaine sporting a Superman button over her small right breast. Place where she told Doris, among other things, that she'd once made love to a friend of Harriet's, Sherry, a middle-aged blonde woman with an expensive, white, four-door Lincoln convertible, a woman in her late fifties, a widow. Lou made a face at the telling that had something to do with her not liking "all that flesh." When she was drunk enough it had seemed like the right thing, a challenge. Doris thought about how much Sherry must have wanted sex, even from Lou. She must have been drunk. Doris could see her although she didn't want to.

Rooms number 5 and 7, you and I would never forget them.

At 813 Beach Avenue. Three bottom steps. Midnight. We sit there together. You, drunk. Nine stone steps and a bannister made of a metal pipe that divides the steps. Two rectangular stone columns stand at either side of the steps; matching drainpipes from the roof attach to the side of each of the stone columns. A gate of wood separates the stairs from the porch and the entrance to the house, its designer a lover of compartmentalization.

I return to this place again and again where something occurred you couldn't explain. A conversation. The odor of someone's pheromones mixes with the smell of alcohol, tobacco, and sadness. The knowing that this person is wounded, that her wounds mix with yours while you are talking or being silent together in a room. Some of the boundaries between you fall away.

In Chinese Medicine, the shen, which is housed in the heart, is affected by insults, humiliation and betrayal. The shen is easily broken. It is possible to mend the shen, though it is not easy.

She used to like the way it felt to come home to Kate after having sex with Lois because she felt depraved and pleased about how it felt to feel depraved. Degraded, sexy. Three lovers; no problem. She could do it. She was high on it. She told Kate she was going to the library to do her grad school assigments. Got them done at top speed. Then the train to Lois's and they'd have the afternoon to spend on the couch in the living room. First they'd talk, Lois about Sparky, her roommate who was her ex-lover, and Sparky's latest AA stories, and about Barbara, the new lover Sparky had discovered at an AA meeting, a handsome, older woman, an editor at a publishing house.

Lois's stories weren't interesting, but they helped pass the time and to draw them together, something the few furtive phonecalls between visits didn't accomplish. They'd have sex on the couch, Lois scarcely having to do much work because Doris was so ready for her, or, rather, for sex. They'd talk a little, tease each other, joke, talk a little more. Then Lois would make love to her, she'd have a huge orgasm in what seemed like a short time, the best she'd ever have. Lois was so big, she didn't have to do much with her body; whatever little she did had a terrific effect on Doris. Then Doris would stroke Lois's body; they'd kiss for a while; she'd make love to Lois; it was always good; she liked Lois best then.

Doris thought if she was going to have a second lover, she

might as well have a third; she had the appetite for it, and more. A hunger, really.

She had read in a book on social anthropology by Helen Fisher, *The Anatomy of Love*, the analysis by a Kung woman of the Kalahari Desert in southern Africa of her sexual journeying, included in the chapter under the general heading "Adultery."

Doris was pleased and intrigued by the woman's description, articulating as it did the impossibility of being satisfied with just one person because different people had different qualities, and if you did not feel taken care of by one person, others could take up the slack.

Not being taken care of created feelings that harmed the liver and heart, contracted the kidneys, damaged the shen. Not being taken care of could create wind, disease, and of course, change. Being taken care of, even if it meant by more than one person, was better than not being taken care of at all and fretting or obsessing about it. Here was the woman's statement. Reading it, Doris could feel the woman's sense of well-being, her good shen, as it would be described in Chinese Medicine.

"There are many kinds of work a woman has to do, and she should have lovers wherever she goes. If she goes somewhere to visit and she is alone, then someone there will give her beads, someone else will give her meat, and someone else will give her other food. When she returns to her village, she will have been well taken care of."

Doris had gotten the idea from the gay men she knew, from their stories, their sexual adventures, having sex in the bushes in Central Park, sometimes with three or four men every night; they loved it, loved relating their adventures to her; she never had to ask, they would just begin to spill out the tale of the night before. She thought she'd go out and have adventures like that; it intrigued her, why not?

My body started out simple and perfect.

Later I learned to dance in planes. I was built low to the ground, the rhythm, the music were all that I needed to take me.

Like the figures in the etchings of Albrecht Dürer inhabit the planes of the page surface, or the way they do in the early dances of Paul Taylor.

Like the Early Christians worked in the planes of the Circus Maximus between gladiators.

My work is about unraveling.

Before Kate there had been Alice. And D.

D. was a friend of a friend. I forget how we met, but we slept together almost immediately.

D. was a _____. After her day job—she had trouble keeping a job—she did piece work at home for extra money, addressing envelopes for companies that paid by the envelope.

She lived in a one-room efficiency uptown; I lived in a furnished room in the Village; we decided we would live in her apartment but that I would not give up my room. Just to try things out. Soon after we met.

We ate supper together at the same time each evening; we slept; we ate the identical breakfast; we went to work. D's frequent and favorite topic of conversation was the loss of Renee, the true love of her life. She had not gotten over it; she would not, she did not have to be urged to pull out snapshots of the diminutive smiling woman with dark curly hair who sold furniture at a fancy department store. After meeting Renee, and knowing herself to be rootless and often out of a job, D. had decided to join the Army to get structure, a steady paycheck and maybe learn a trade. Afterwards, she planned to come back to Renee who would be waiting for her and they would live happily ever after.

But Alice moved in swiftly after D.'s departure and offered Renee the solidity of a relationship with her; she was a solid citizen after all, wasn't going off anywhere, one could depend on her. When D. got out of the Army and wanted Renee to come back to her, Renee would not. "And why should she," D. said morosely, "what do I have to offer her?" In order to get out of the Army, which proved rigorous and confining in the wrong ways, D. had to marry a gay man named Enrique Martinez whom she had since lost touch with.

Listening to the stories of D. and the characters in her life was like watching a movie or play that bore no connection to me, but the plots had something to them, a life different from mine and from anything that I knew.

It was clear to me from the beginning that Alice's true interest was not me but Renee, even as she flirted with me on the side. So I began to go out with D., who seemed more immediately promising as a lover. Right away it was understood that we would sleep together; there were no preliminaries.

D. was a sad woman of about thirty-five, of Irish and Spanish parentage with dark blond hair, dark skin, blue eyes and a strong, stocky body that looked as if it was made for work.

The first night we made love, which she did very expertly, I tried to make love to her in precisely the way I thought she had made love to me. My sexual experience was limited.

She smiled at me afterwards. "You're something else," she said, "you stopped me from coming three times. On purpose! Didn't want me to come too soon, did you?" She was taking for granted I had known what I was doing, and, moreover, that I'd done it on purpose to prolong her pleasure when I'd simply changed rhythms to accommodate myself; it had been accidental; she hadn't known the difference and I didn't tell her.

One Saturday night, Bill Ream who lived on Gay Street, just behind Eighth Street and Sixth Avenue, threw a party that lasted until nearly dawn. Almost everybody ended up staying over. It was afternoon by the time we got up and ate a greasy breakfast of bacon, fried onions and eggs cooked in a mammoth pan by several people. D. and I, who had slept in the three-quarter bed in Bill's alcove, had sex *de rigueur* before we got up after too little sleep and left to go home to her apartment

Blinking in the bright sunlight, we emerged, rumpled and sleepy at four in the afternoon, feeling like moles.

It was Easter Sunday, the streets alive with people dressed in bright new clothes. Pushing our way through the crowd to get to the uptown subway, we seemed alien to each other and to the masses of people who filled the street. Now D. seemed a total stranger and I dreaded going to her apartment. There was nothing for us to say, nothing to talk about. I would feel imprisoned with D., yet I was not ready to go home to my furnished room. I felt separated from everyone that I knew, and especially from the crowds of people bent on celebrating Easter and partaking of a ritual about which I knew nothing. I imagined they were going to church to renew their faith in the Resurrection and thus in themselves and their lives.

That Easter morning after making love with D., I'd risen, emptied, bodily and spiritually. Caught in the *tohubohu* of Alice's, Bill's, and D.'s life, I felt marked by each of them, though they were not the life I was seeking; indeed, I did not know who I was or what it was that I sought.

Do I not at the age of six dream myself crawling over the nude body of my second-grade teacher, both of us in ecstasy, she a grown woman, I a child?

Have I not at fifteen fallen and cracked my back, been gripped in pain for months and years, never to speak of it, just bear it, only to rise, reborn, one of the many deaths and rebirths I am to experience over the course of my existence?

My body at twenty: enough power to leap higher into the air than anyone. Enough energy to die with.

My body at twenty-one, neck covered with Kate's hickeys and proud of them. "Who did that to you?" "My boyfriend."

My body at twenty-three: I am called on for jury duty, they cannot believe I am more than seventeen, maybe eighteen years old.

My body at nineteen: I stay up all night with Bill and his friends, go home to shower and change clothes to catch the train to Flatbush to the last stop, wait in line for the bus to the gay section of the beach, which is known as Jacob Riis Park. I envy the boys their freedom, their sensuality, their promiscuity, the public-ness of their lives, their ability to be exactly who they are, their gay slang which I pick up fast and keep.

When I am twenty-four I work with two black women. Chloe is married, with a small daughter, Olga, unmarried, with a twelve-year-old son. They are both tall, willowy, dark brown, handsome and always together. Their bodies seem to undulate when they walk; they walk and talk wonderfully slowly.

Chloe speaks often of Roger, her husband, their daughter Emily and their happy family life. Olga speaks little of her life outside the job except to mention the problems Eric, her son, has behaving himself at school, and the fact that if she did not have her job to go to each day, she would not know what to do with herself. She has lived with a woman named Cerine, whom she sees when either of them is lonely enough. The next day at lunch when she mentions the visit she always yawns and then stretches.

One evening, a woman in my department has invited all of us to her house for dinner. Chloe does not join us. I find myself sitting next to Olga on the couch. Chloe, Olga and I have spent many lunch hours together, eating, laughing and talking—when I am not too seized with anxiety because of something Kate has done or said. It is the height of summer. The air conditioner and all the lights are on which causes a fuse to blow. In the darkness I feel Olga's hand uncurl in my lap with languid but specific purpose. For a moment I do not understand its presence. When the lights go back on, she smiles at me her lazy smile. I smile back. I don't acknowledge her gesture but I've discovered that I'm not easily available for casual stroking, something I haven't thought of before.

My body at thirty-three. The doctor saying, this is the way life is. From now on, everything will go downwards for you physically. I refuse to believe her; I think she is dead wrong; I have enough energy to die with.

My body at thirty-six. I walk down the street with two women I have become friendly with. Both are teachers at the University. One of them, Johanna, the more serious and dignified of the pair half jokingly says to me, "I wouldn't mind poking *you* in the belly."

I think I am charmed. I do not seek it. From Olga to Johanna Smith, everyone loves me.

It is Portia Forrest I am besotted with.

I write love letters to her in the voices of the ice cubes in the freezer of her refrigerator, her living room chairs and couch, her bedclothes and sheets, her toothbrush. I tell her how much she is missed while she is away on a business trip. I send this letter, meant to amuse and impress her with the depths of my love, so it will be waiting for her on the day that she arrives home.

She never mentions it.

She nevertheless comes to visit me where I live in a small suburban town called Streambank. Her visit makes me unbelievably happy. Ardent about fishing, and an authority on fishing tackle, she also plays the flute. She works as a therapist at the counseling center of the University. She loves a good steak, plenty of cigarettes, booze, pastries and chocolates. She is high-voiced and shy-spoken, something you don't quite expect from such a tall, statuesque woman. We have little to say to each other but I do not care, I want her presence. She neither stays away nor comes close. I decide that she is afraid of me and of my passion for her. She freezes at the thought of lovemaking, the mention of sex, the idea of the body. I am too besotted to know what to do.

Sometimes I think I would have devoured her and thrown away the husk.

My body at forty, hiding from the sun in the rocky crevices of Monhegan Island's rocky cliffs. I am, from a crouched position, animal-like, taking one risky leap after the other from the edge of one cliff to another, my feet as bare as the day I am born. I am as invincible now as the day I was twenty; nothing can stop me.

*   *   *

She has looked up in Oriental astrology books the meaning of her elemental sign. The books say she is a number five, which represents the element of Earth. Its natural phenomenon is primal power.

The status of number five is different from that of the other seven numbers, and is considered to be by far the most powerful. In its primal power, it rises upwards from the earth possessing both creative and destructive capabilities. Five is the human being at the center of her world with the power to create and destroy; there is choice, one can do either. The most powerful of the signs, five is represented within the body at dead center where the spleen and stomach are found; without these organs digestion cannot take place, there is no life.

It is impossible to go against the power of five; if it decides to go after something, it gets what it wants. The creative or destructive potential within the individual must be in balance in order for the five power to be harnessed and constructively used.

Five must constantly renew itself.

My still-invincible body at forty-nine is a mass of scars, hidden and visible.

Healed scars are what my body is made of.

Left foot, two broken toes, healed.

Two broken fingers, right index, left pinky, healed.

Painful feet, healed. My macrobiotic teachers laugh aloud when I tell them the podiatrist has explained that the pain in my feet is caused by the flesh of my footpads being worn away from having walked around on them too much. They say the pain is caused by stagnant energy in the meridians located in the feet. They turn out to be right.

My numb, smallest left toe, healed.

The numbness in my right groin, healed.

My neck injuries, my back injuries, my desire to float through the trees behind the New York Public Library, healed.

*   *   *

She lay on the table underneath Sonia's hands. Her body passed before her closed eyes in a pose she knew well. She was standing, hands on hips, seen from the back, wearing shorts and a striped polo shirt, her hair blond, and in braids. It wasn't the photograph that passed through her, it was the body itself, her body, fifteen, in its flesh, its newness, its excitement, its despair, its teeth, its arms, its menstrual blood, its bowels, its tumultous orgasms.

When she was fifteen, the world was as open as she and now it was happening again. She could taste the flesh of her back, her thighs, her chest, her ankles and toes; it was firm, solid, it shimmered and rocked through her arms and ankles, chest and shoulders; her old self, her new self, melded and passed, one into the other. She could feel herself descend into space, feel it open before her, a swirled and moving firmament soft as cotton, what the sky must feel like as you go through, dive through, it parts, gently and lightly and then draws you further into itself. Everything that would happen to her afterwards was part of the swirling midnight and purple-blue firmament; her injuries and wounds, even the scars that had not yet happened; the hornet's sting on her left wrist as she lay in a daze in the heat on a deck chair in the midst of the overgrown grasses of the old farm she had lived in for seven years, the grasses nearly as tall as she was, difficult to part them to get through to the next path, which was overgrown even further; she got through them, her hands cut, her hands scraped and scratched. This farm she had rented for seven years, 508 Bethlehem Pike, her car parked on the shoulder of the road one winter night smashed to smithereens by a drunk driver who leaned down to retrieve his cigarette from the floor, she at home asleep in bed with the cops ringing her phone to wake her and tell her her car had just been totalled in an accident; her wounds, her injuries, they filled, they piled onto her body, inside and outside until she knew that her body was the map of her life, the roads on which her body had taken her, this number five will that would not, could not be gainsaid. Traveled, the fifteen-year-old Doris limber and happy in summer, her games, all of her stories before her, she would be lost in her play, her life awash in the richness, the lightness, the fire of summer, its glory, the leap over the tall metal fence with spikes at the top that called to her to leap over them; she had made it, had easily made it, but just barely.

It had begun in summer, her life had begun then. It was caught then, summer's organ, the heart, as if in the whorl of the time when the firmament draws her, and her scars—each of them—layered on her body and spirit, the lump in her breast, nearly as large as the breast itself, making that breast a shape different from the other; the nipple became filled with the old scars of her anger and rage, it became hard.

Her fingers: distorted, filled with the scars of her obsessions and rage.

Her scars: everywhere, visible, invisible, she knew them by heart; she was nothing but a map of her scars and the places they'd come from and taken her.

Her breast where the lump had grown and changed its shape so many times in the place where her father had cupped his hand that one evening, reached into her heart and created her heart's first hardness, the wound that would continue to grow in the dark, and was never going to leave. He had died, the artifacts of his life, his notebooks and tragic poems, its glories, its highs, its lows, its dramas, bequeathed to her, wasted. She avoided the artifacts of her father for she traced the subterranean waters, the stopped stream in her body to the mudded backup of his gifts, wanted and unwanted.

She could see the spectre, the outline, drawn in the air, of her body, transparent and flattened against the sky, the moon and stars visible inside it, like the graphite and wax crayon drawing by Artaud on a picture postcard—she'd mailed it to R.—"les illusions de l'âme"—the illusions of the soul—thinking it was a picture both of R. and herself, in each other's mind's eye. To her, somehow, it was a message to herself; she did not know what it was to R.

She knew it would happen again if it had to: the agony and the delight, the translucence. The ways she'd been stitched-up and cut and cut again. The way that some of the scars had been touched in desire by women who wanted her, wanted to touch even her scars. She dreamt this.

The wellspring of desire in the depths of her number five soul, her oneness, her celestial scarred hands ready to touch someone in desire.

The way things wrote themselves on her.

She would not have to relearn the seasons; the calendar *was* her, she was the time-reckoning of her life, the myth of herself in each joint, in the bunion on her big toe, her synovial fluids, the scarred right elbow.

Two broken toes, left foot.

Two broken fingers, one on each hand.

Myopia: poring over the pages of books in the dark they'd warned her you'll spoil your eyes you'll have to wear glasses with lenses as thick as stove lids don't read in the dark.

Her gold tooth visible in her mouth when she smiled from the long time she had been too poor to go to a dentist and chewed Dentyne gum instead, the poor man's dentist; she'd always joked about it.

The scars glittered and flashed as if they were the stars and the moon. Nighttime or day, she was her firmament, floating, the universe humming inside her, the dream of herself her own continent on which everything went on inscribing itself.

About the Author

A native New Yorker, Alexandra Grilikhes has taught Creative Writing, Writing Memoir, and Women Studies at the University of the Arts for more than two decades. A long-time innovator in literary broadcasting, she hosted the only literary programs in Philadelphia, on public radio, for ten years. Director of the University of Pennsylvania's Annenberg School of Communications Library, she organized and produced four groundbreaking international annual festivals of Films by Women at the Annenberg Center for the Arts.

A dance and performance art writer, critic, and author of nine small-press collections of poetry, the most recent of which is *Shaman Body* (1996), she was a 1999 Pushcart Prize nominee in fiction. Her stories, essays and poetry are widely published in such places as *Pleiades, Grand Street, Spillway, Fuel, The Seattle Review, Fish Drum, The Lesbian Review of Books, Pangolin Papers,* and *River Styx.* She is editor and publisher of the eleven-year-old independent, national literary/arts journal *American Writing: A Magazine.*